THE MYSTERY OF THE GREEN RAY

By William Le Queux

Originally published in 1915

The Mystery of the Green Ray

© 2011 Resurrected Press
www.ResurrectedPress.com

Published by Resurrected Press

This classic book was handcrafted by Resurrected Press. Resurrected Press is dedicated to bringing high quality classic books back to the readers who enjoy them. These are not scanned versions of the originals, but, rather, quality checked and edited books meant to be enjoyed!

Please visit ResurrectedPress.com to view our entire catalogue!

ISBN 13: 978-1-937022-00-6

Printed in the United States of America

FOREWORD

The Mystery of the Green Ray is set on the eve of World War I. The years leading up to the war had seen a host of novels about German spies, invasion plans and secret weapons, and it is into this category that this book fits. Le Queux, capitalizing on this trend has given us a story about the development of such a secret weapon and the attempts to thwart it by a pair of young men who stumble into the affair.

World War I saw the introduction of a number of new and terrible weapons to warfare, the airplane, the tank, and poison gas to name a few. With the rapid progress in science and technology at the end of the nineteenth and early twentieth centuries, it was only to be expected by the public that such marvels should be turned to deadly purpose. Yet, that science was still imperfectly understood. Electricity and radiation were relatively recent discoveries just becoming familiar to the general public. The possibility of a secret weapon as described in the book, while viewed as unlikely today, would have seemed quite plausible to a generation just graduating from gaslights and horse drawn carriages.

One interesting feature of the book is the view of Americans on the part of the British public. Until the U.S. came into the war, there was a great deal of resentment and suspicion of Americans. Because of the large population of Germans in the American population there was some doubt, especially early in the war, as to which side the U.S. would come in on if she did enter the war. It took the notorious Zimmerman telegram in which the German's promised restoration of the American southwest to Mexico and the sinking of the *Lusitania* to bring the U.S. onto the side of the British and French.

Le Queue was a master of the form, writing some hundred and fifty novels of suspense and intrigue. Resurrected Press is happy to bring *The Mystery of the Green Ray* to its readers for their enjoyment.

About the Author

William Tufnell Le Queux (July 2, 1884-October 13, 1927) was an Anglo-French author. Born in London, he was educated in Europe. He worked as an editor and reporter for various British magazines and newspapers before turning to writing full time. He wrote numerous novels, mostly in the mystery and suspense genres, of which the best known may be *The Invasion of 1910*. In addition to writing, he was also involved in pioneering radio experiments.

Greg Fowlkes
Editor-In-Chief
Resurrected Press
www.ResurrectedPress.com

TABLE OF CONTENTS

Chapter 1: Beside Still Waters

The youth in the multi-coloured blazer laughed.

"You'd have to come and be a nurse," he suggested.

"Oh, I'd go as a drummer-boy. I'd look fine in uniform, wouldn't I?" the waitress simpered in return.

Dennis Burnham swallowed his liqueur in one savage gulp, pushed back his chair, and rose from the table.

"Silly young ass," he said, in a voice loud enough for the object of his wrath to hear. "Let's get outside."

The four of us rose, paid our bill, and went out, leaving the youth and his flippant companions to themselves. For it was Bank Holiday, August the third, 1914, and I think, though it was the shortest and most uneventful of all our river "annuals," it is the one which we are least likely to forget. On the Saturday Dennis, Jack Curtis, Tommy Evans and myself had started from Richmond on our yearly trip up the river. Even as we sat in the two punts playing bridge, moored at our first camping-place below Kingston Weir, disquieting rumours reached us in the form of excited questions from the occupants of passing craft. And now, as we rose from the dinner-table at the Magpie, Sunbury, two days later, it seemed that war was inevitable.

"What I can't understand," growled Dennis, as we stepped into one of the punts and paddled idly across to the lock, "is how any young idiot can treat the whole thing as a terrific joke. If we go to war with Germany—and it seems we must—it's going to be——Good Heavens! who knows what it's going to be!"

"Meaning," said Tom, who never allowed any thought to remain half-expressed, "meaning that we are not prepared, and they are. We have to step straight into the ring untrained to meet an opponent who has been getting ready night and day for the Lord knows how many years."

"Still, you know," said Jack, who invariably found the bright spot in everything, "we never did any good as a nation until we were pushed."

"We shall be pushed this time," I replied; "and if we do go to war, we shall all be wanted."

"And wanted at once," Tom added.

"Which brings me to the point which most concerns us," said Dennis, with a serious face. "What are *we* going to do?"

"It seems to me," I replied, "that there is only one thing we can do. If the Government declare war, it is in your cause and mine; and who is to fight our battles but you and me?"

"That's it, old man, exactly," said Dennis. "We must appear in person, as you lawyers would say. I'm afraid there's not the slightest hope of peace being maintained now; and, indeed, in view of the circumstances, I should prefer to say there is not the slightest fear of it. We can't honourably keep out, so let us hope we shall step in at once."

Jack's muttered "hear hear" spoke for us all, and there was silence for a minute or two. My thoughts were very far away from the peaceful valley of the Thames; they had flown, in fact, to a still more peaceful glen in the Western Highlands—but of that anon. I fancy the others, too, were thinking of something far removed from the ghastly horror of war. Jack was sitting with an open cigarette-case in his hand, gazing wistfully at the bank to which we had moored the boat. There was a "little girl" in the question. Poor chap; I knew exactly what he was thinking; he had my sympathy! The silence became uncomfortable, and it was Jack who broke it.

"Give me a match, Tommy," he exclaimed suddenly, "and don't talk so much." Tom, who had not spoken a word for several minutes, produced the matches from a capacious pocket, and we all laughed rather immoderately at the feeble sally.

"As to talking," said Tom, when our natural equanimity had been restored, "you all seem to be leaving me to say what we all know has to be said. And that is, what is the next item on the programme?"

"I think we had certainly better decide——" Dennis began.

"You old humbug!" exclaimed Tom. "You know perfectly well that we've all decided what we are going to do. It is merely the question of putting it in words. In some way or other we intend to regard the case of Rex *v.* Wilhelm as one in which we personally are concerned. Am I right?"

"Scored a possible," said Jack, who had quite recovered his spirits.

"In which case," Tom continued, "we don't expect to be of much assistance to our King and country if we go gallivanting up to Wallingford, as originally intended. The question, therefore, remains, shall we go back by train—if we can find the station here—or shall we punt back to Richmond?"

"I don't think we need worry about that," said Dennis. "I vote we go back by river; it will be more convenient in every way, and we can leave the boats at Messums. If things are not so black as we think they are we can step on board again with a light heart, or four light hearts, if you prefer it, and start again. What do you say, Ron?"

"I should prefer to paddle back," I replied. "It would be a pity to break up our party immediately. I don't want to be sentimental, or anything of that sort, but you chaps will agree that we have had some very jolly times together in the past, and if we are all going to take out our naturalisation papers in the Atkins family, it is just possible that we—well, we may not be all together again next year."

"And you, Jack?" asked Dennis.

"Oh, down stream for me," said young Curtis, with what was obviously an effort at his usual light-hearted manner. "Think of all the beer we've got left." But the laugh with which he accompanied his remark was not calculated to deceive any of us, and I am afraid my clumsy speech had set him thinking again. So we went "ashore," and had a nightcap at the Magpie, where the flippant youth was announcing to an admiring circle that if he had half a dozen pals to go with him he wouldn't mind joining the army himself! Having scoured the village in an unavailing attempt to round up half a pound of butter, we put off down stream, and spent the night in the beautiful backwater. No one suggested cards after supper, and we lay long into the night discussing, as thousands of other people all over the country were probably discussing, conscription, espionage, martial law, the possibilities of invasion, and the probable duration of the war. I doubt very much if we should have gone to sleep at all had we been able to foresee the events which the future, in its various ways, held in store for each of us. But, as it was, we plunged wholeheartedly into what Tommy Evans described as "Life's new interest." We positively thrilled at the prospect of army life.

"Think of it," said Jack enthusiastically, "open air all the time. Nothing to worry about, no work to do, only manual labour. Why, it's going to be one long holiday. Hang it! I've laid drain-pipes on a farm—for fun!"

It was past one o'clock when we got out supper. And our appetites lost nothing by the prospect of hardships which we treated rather lightly, since we entirely failed to appreciate their seriousness. Jack's visions of storming ramparts at the point of the bayonet merely added flavour to his amazing collation of cold beef, ham, brawn, cold fowl, and peaches and cream, with which he insisted on winding-up at nearly two in the morning. He would have shouted with laughter had you told him that in less than three weeks he would be dashing through the enemy's lines with despatches on a red-hot motor-cycle. And Tommy—poor old Tommy—well, I fancy he would have been just as cheerful, dear old chap, had he known the fate that was in store. For to him was to fall the lot which, of all others, everyone—rich and poor alike—understands. There is no need for me to repeat the story. Even in the rush of a war which has already brought forward some thousands of heroes, the reader will remember the glorious exploit of Corporal Thomas Evans, in which he won the D.C.M., and also, unfortunately,

gave his life for his country. It is sufficient to say
that three men in particular will ever cherish his
memory as that of a loyal friend, a cheery comrade, a
clean, honest, straightforward Englishman through
and through.

As for Dennis and myself—but I am coming to
that.

Having finished our early morning supper, we
turned in for a few hours' sleep, Jack and Tommy in
one boat, Dennis and I in the other. But before we
did so we stood up, as well as we could under our
canvas roof, and drank "The King"; and I fancy that
in the mind of each of us there was more than one
other name silently coupled with that toast. Then,
for the first time in my memory of our intimacy
together, we solemnly shook hands before turning in.
But, try as I would, I couldn't sleep. For a long time I
lay there, in the beautiful silence of the night, my
thoughts far away, sleep farther away still.
Presently I grovelled for my tobacco-pouch.

"Restless, Ron?" Dennis asked, himself evidently
quite wide awake.

"Can't sleep at all," I answered. "But don't let me
disturb you."

"You're not disturbing me, old man. I can't sleep
either. Let's light the lamp and smoke."

Accordingly we fished out our pipes and relighted
the acetylene lamp, which hung from the middle
hoop. Jack turned over in his sleep.

"Put out the light, old fellow. Not a cab'net
meeting, y'know," he murmured drowsily. And by
way of compromise I pulled the primitive draught
curtain between the two boats, and as I sat up to do
so I noticed with a start that Dennis wore a worried

look I had never seen before. I lay back, got my pipe going, and waited for him to speak.

"I wonder," he said presently, through the clouds of smoke that hung imprisoned beneath our shallow roof—"I wonder if there would have been any war if the Germans smoked Jamavana?"

"What's worrying you, Den?" I asked, ignoring his question.

"Worrying me? Why, nothing. I've got nothing to worry about. What about you, though? I don't want to butt in on your private affairs, but you've a lot more to be worried about than I have."

"I? Oh, nonsense, Dennis," I protested.

"None of that with me, Ron. You know what I mean. There's no point in either of us concealing things. This war is going to make a big difference to you and Myra McLeod. Now, tell me all about it. What do you mean to do, and everything?"

"There isn't much to tell you. You know all about it. We're not engaged. Old General McLeod objects to our engagement on account of my position. Of course, he's quite right. He's very nice about it, and he's always kindness itself to me. You know, of course, that he and my father were brother officers? Myra and I have been chums since she was four. We love each other, and she would be content to wait, but, in the meantime—well, you know my position. I can only describe it in the well-worn phrases, 'briefless barrister' and 'impecunious junior.' There's a great deal of truth in the weak old joke, Dennis, about the many that are called and the few that are briefed. Of course the General is right. He says that I ought to leave Myra absolutely alone, and neither write to her nor see her, and give her a chance to

meet someone else, and all that—someone who could
keep her among her own set. But I tried that once for
three months; I didn't answer her letters, or write to
her, and I worried myself to death very nearly about
it. But at the end of the three months she came up to
town to see what it was all about. Gad, how glad I
was to see her!"

"I bet you were," said Dennis, sympathetically.
"But what d'you mean by telling me you'd got
nothing to worry about? Now that you're just getting
things going nicely, and look like doing really well,
along comes this wretched war, and you join the
army, and such practice as you have goes to the
devil. It's rotten luck, Ronnie, rotten luck."

"It is a bit," I admitted with a sigh. My little bit of
hard-earned success had meant a lot to me.

"Still," said Dennis, "you've got a thundering lot
to be thankful for too. To begin with, she'll wait for
you, and then, if necessary, marry on twopence-
halfpenny a year, and make you comfortable on it
too. As far as her father is concerned, she's very
devoted to him, and would never do anything to
annoy him if she could possibly help it, as I easily
spotted the night we dined with them at the Carlton.
But she's made up her mind to be Mrs. Ronald
Ewart sooner or later; that I *will* swear!"

"I'm very glad to hear you say so," I answered,
"but the thing that worries me, of course, is the
question as to whether I have any right to let this go
on. If war is declared——"

"Which it will be," said Dennis.

"Well, then, my practice goes to the devil, as you
say. How long after the war is it going to be before I
could marry one of Myra's maids, let alone Myra?

And, supposing, of course, that I use the return half of my ticket, so to speak, and come back safe and sound, my own prospects will be infinitely worse than they were before the war. The law, after all, is a luxury, and no one will have a great deal of money for luxuries by the time we have finished with it and wiped Germany off the map. Besides, if there's no money about, there's nothing to go to law over. So there you are, or, rather, there I am."

"What do you intend to do, then?" my friend asked.

"I shall go up to Scotland to-morrow night—well, of course, it's to-night, I should say—and see her—and—and——"

"Yes—well, and——"

"Oh, and tell her that it must be all—all over. I shall say that the war will make all the difference, that I must join the army, and that she must consider herself free to marry someone else, and that, as in any case I might never come back, I think it's the best thing for us both that she should consider herself free, and—er—and—and consider herself free," I ended weakly.

"Just like that?" asked Dennis, with a twinkle in his eye.

"I shall try and put it fairly formally to her," I said, "because, of course, I must appear to be sincere about it. I must try and think out some way of making her imagine I want it broken off for reasons of my own."

Dennis laughed softly.

"You delicious, egotistical idiot," he said. "You don't really imagine that you could persuade anyone you met for the first time even that you're not in

love. By all means do what you think is right, Ron. I
wouldn't dissuade you for the world. Tell her that
she is free. Tell her why you are setting her free, and
I'll be willing to wager my little all that you two
ridiculous young people will find yourselves tied
tighter together than ever. By all means do your best
to be a good little boy, Ronald, and do what you
conceive to be your duty."

"You needn't pull my leg about it," I said, though
somewhat half-heartedly.

"I'm not pulling your leg, as you put it," Dennie
answered, in a more serious tone. "If ever I saw
honesty and truth and love and loyalty looking out of
a girl's eyes, that girl is Myra McLeod."

"Thank you for that, Den," I answered simply.
There was little sentiment between us. Thank
heaven, there was something more.

"And so you see, you lucky dog, you'll go out to
the front, and come back loaded with honours and
blushes, and marry the girl of your dreams, and live
happy ever after." And Dennis sighed.

"Why the sigh?" I asked. "Oh, come now," I added,
suddenly remembering. "Fair exchange, you know.
You haven't told me what was worrying you."

"My dear old fellow, don't be ridiculous, there's
nothing worrying me."

I pressed him to no purpose. He refused to admit
that he had a care in the world, and so we fell to
talking of matters connected with the routine of
army life, how long we should be before we got to the
front, the sport we four should have in our rest time
behind the trenches, our determination to stick
together at all costs, etc. Suddenly Dennis sat bolt
upright.

"Gad!" he cried savagely, "if you beggars weren't going, I could stick it. But you three leaving me behind, it's——"

"Leaving you behind?" I echoed in astonishment. "But why, old man? Aren't you coming too?"

"I hope so," said Dennis bitterly; "I hope so with all my heart, and I shall have a jolly good shot at it. But I know what it will be, worse luck."

"But why, Dennis?" I asked again. "I don't understand."

"Of course you don't," he replied, "but you've got your own troubles, and there's no point in worrying about me, in any case."

I begged him to tell me; I pleaded our old friendship, and the fact that I had taken him into my confidence in the various vicissitudes of my own love affair. It struck me at the time that it was I who should have been indebted to him for his patient sympathy and help; and here he was, poor old fellow, with a real, live trouble of his own, refusing to bother me with it.

"So you've just got to own up, old man," I finished.

"Oh, it's really nothing," said Dennis miserably. "I'm a crock, that's all. A useless hulk of unnecessary lumber."

"How, my dear chap?" I asked incredulously. Here was Dennis Burnham, who had put up a record for the mile in our school days, and lifted the public school's middle-weight pot, a champion swimmer, a massive young man of six-foot-two in his socks, calling himself a crock.

"You remember that summer we did the cruise from Southampton to Stranraer?"

"Heavens! yes," I exclaimed, "and we capsized the cutter in the Solway, and you were laid up in a farmhouse at Whithorn with rheumatic fever. Am I ever likely to forget it?"

"I'm not, anyway," said Dennis, ruefully. "That rheumatic fever left me with a weak heart. I strained it rowing up at Oxford, you remember, and that fever business put the last touches on it for all practical purposes."

"Are you sure, old man?" I asked. It seemed impossible that a great big chap like Dennis, the picture of health, should have anything seriously wrong with him.

"I'm dead sure, Ron; I wish I weren't. Not that it matters much, of course; but just now, when one has a chance to do something decent for one's Motherland and justify one's existence, it hits a bit hard."

"Is it serious?" I asked—"really serious?"

"Sufficient to bar me from joining you chaps, though I'll see if I can sneak past the doctor. You remember about three weeks ago we were to have played a foursome out at Hendon, and I didn't turn up? I said afterwards that I had been called out of town, and had quite forgotten to wire."

"Which was extremely unlike you," I interposed; "but go on."

"Well, as a matter of fact, I was on my way. I was a bit late, and when I got outside Golders Green Tube Station I ran for a 'bus. The rest of the day I spent in the Cottage Hospital. No, I didn't faint. The valve struck, and I simply lay on the pavement a crumpled mass of semi-conscious humanity till they carted me off on the ambulance. It's the fourth time it's happened."

"Of course you had good advice?" I asked anxiously.

"Heavens! yes," he exclaimed; "any amount of the best. And they all say the same thing—rest, be careful, no sudden excitement, no strain, and I may live for ever—a creaking door."

"My dear old Den," I said, for I was deeply touched. "Why didn't you tell me?"

"Plenty of worries of your own, old man," he answered, more cheerfully; "and, besides, it would have spoiled everything. You fellows would have been nursing me behind my back, to use an Irishism, and trying to prevent my noticing it. You know as well as I do that if you had known I should have been a skeleton at the feast."

"You must promise me two things," I said presently. "One is that you won't try to join the army; there is sure to be a rush of recruits in the next few days, and the doctors will be flurried, and may skip through their work roughshod. The other is that you will take care of yourself, run no risks, and do nothing rash while we are away."

The first he refused. He said he must do what he could to get through, if only to satisfy his conscience; but he made me the second promise, and solemnly gave me his word that he would do nothing that would put him in any danger. Then at last, at his suggestion, we turned in; he insisted that I had an all-night journey in front of me. And so eventually I fell asleep, saddened by the knowledge of my friend's trouble, but somewhat relieved that I had extracted from him a promise to take care of himself.

Little did I dream that he would break his promise to save one who was dearer to me than life itself, or that I should owe all my present and future happiness to poor old Dennis's inability to join the army. Truly, as events were to prove, "he did his bit."

CHAPTER II. THE MAN GOING NORTH

We "made" Richmond about half-past eleven, and completed the necessary arrangements for the housing of the boats and the disposal of our superfluous fodder, as Jack called it, for by this time we had all made up our minds that the war was inevitable.

The bustle of mobilisation had already taken possession of the streets, and as we stepped out of Charing Cross Station we stumbled into a crowd of English Bluejackets and Tommies and French reservists in Villiers Street. We parted for the afternoon, each to attend to his private affairs, and arranged to meet again at the Grand Hotel Grill Room for an early dinner, as I had to catch the 7.55 from King's Cross.

I dashed out to Hampstead to my flat, and packed the necessary wearing apparel, taking care to include my fly-book and my favourite split-cane trout rod in my kit. I should only be in Scotland for a couple of days, but I knew that I should be fishing with Myra at least one of them, and no borrowed rod is a patch on one's own tried favourite. I snatched an half-hour or so to write to the few relatives I have and tell them that I was joining the army after a hurried visit to Scotland to say good-bye to Myra. And then I got my kit to Dennis's rooms in Panton Street, Haymarket, just in time to have a chat with him before we joined the others at the Grand Hotel. I found him hopefully getting things ready for a long absence, sorting out unanswered letters, putting away papers, etc. On the table was an open copy of a stores catalogue. He had been trying to find suitable presents for his two small step-sisters. Dennis invariably thought of himself last of all, and then usually at someone else's request.

"Well, old man," I asked, "how do you feel about it now?"

"Rotten, Ronnie," he replied, with a rueful smile. "I've been on the 'phone to my silly doctor chap, and he shouted with laughter at me. Still, I shall have a jolly good shot at it as soon as the thing is definite."

"I only pray to heaven," I said seriously, "that no slipshod fool of a doctor lets you through."

"They won't let me in, old chap; no such luck. It's a ghastly outlook. What on earth am I to do with myself while the war lasts?"

"My dear chap," I exclaimed, "it won't be as bad as all that. There will be thousands of men who won't go to the war. I shan't be surprised if you see very little difference about town even when the war's in full swing. You can't go, although you want to, and it's jolly bad luck, old man. Don't think I don't understand, but, believe me, you won't be the only man left in London by a million or two."

"I know," he said penitently, "I'm grousing and worrying you. Sorry! But I can see you setting out for the Temple in the morning and leaving your house on fire. It wouldn't make it easier simply because you knew you weren't able to do anything to put out the fire. In fact, it would make it a jolly lot worse. Still, we'll cut that and change the subject. When you get back from Invermalluch give me a look up. I expect I shall be here. And, of course, give my kindest regards to Miss McLeod—oh, and the General," he added, as an afterthought.

"I will, indeed," I promised readily, "and I'll wire you the train I'm coming back by. I should like you to meet it, and we can spend the few remaining days I have together. If you don't get past the doctor I should like you to keep your eye on one or two things for me while I'm away."

"Of course, anything you like. The more the merrier," he answered readily; and the poor fellow brightened visibly at the thought of being able to do something for a pal.

We taxied round the corner with my kit, and joined the others at the grill room. They were both in the highest of spirits, Jack, of course, in particular. He had been told that his intimate knowledge of motors and motor-cycles would be of great advantage to him, and he had been advised on all hands to join as a despatch-rider. In imagination he already saw himself up to the most weird pranks on his machine, many of which, much to the gratification of his friends, and just as much to his own astonishment, were proved later to have a solid foundation in fact. Over dinner we discussed the question of applying for commissions.

"Oh, dash it, no," said Jack; "I'm going to Berlin on the old snorter."

"Commissions are off—quite out of the question," Tommy agreed with emphasis. "To begin with, it means waiting, which is absurd; and in the second place I object to any attempt to travel first-class. It's silly and snobbish, to put the kindest construction on it. If I've got to join this excursion I'm willing to go where they like to put me, and if necessary I'll hang on behind."

I record this remark because it was the last that I ever heard poor Tommy Evans make in this connection; and I think the reader will agree it was just what one would have expected of him.

We said good-bye after dinner. They all wanted to come to the station to see me off, but I was anxious to be alone with Dennis.

The others in any case had plenty to do, and I could scarcely let them sacrifice their "last few hours of liberty" to come and see me off. I rather expected that the excitement of the war would have prevented a lot of people travelling, but the reverse was the case. There seemed to be more people than ever on the platform, and I could not get a corner seat even in the Fort William coach. I bundled my things into a carriage and took up as much room as I could, and then Dennis and I strolled about the platform until the train was due to start.

"Strange mixtures of humanity you see on a railway platform," Dennis remarked presently.

"Very," I agreed. "I daresay there are some very curious professions represented here."

"This chap, for instance," said Dennis, indicating a youth in a tweed jacket and flannel trousers. "He might be anything from an M.P.'s private secretary to an artist's model, for all we know. I should say he's a journalist; he knows his way through a crowd as only journalists do."

"A typical Yorkshire cattle-dealer in his Sunday best," I suggested, as we passed another passenger. And so we went the length of the platform making rough guesses as to the professions of my fellow travellers. Suddenly I noticed a tall man, wearing a tweed cap and a long covert-coat, his hands in his pockets, a stumpy cigar stuck in the corner of his mouth. His hair was gray, and his face bore signs of a tough struggle in early youth. His complexion was of that curious gray-yellow one sees frequently in America and occasionally in Denmark—something quite distinct from the bronze-gray of many colonials. I nudged Dennis.

"What did you make of that?" I asked him after we had passed.

"I should be much more interested to know what 'that' made of us," he replied.

"Nothing, I should think," I answered carelessly. "Why, the man's eyes were nearly closed, he was half asleep. I bet he hasn't taken the slightest notice of anyone for the past ten minutes. You could commit a murder under his nose and he wouldn't see it."

"I think not," said Dennis quietly. "I fancy that if you took out a cigarette-case as you passed him he would be able to tell you afterwards how many cigarettes you had left in the case, what brand they were, and what the monogram on the front was. If you've any murders to commit, Ronnie, I should be careful to see that our American friend is some thousands of miles away."

"Good heavens, you old sleuth!" I exclaimed in astonishment. "I never saw a more innocent-looking man in my life."

"I hate innocent people," said Dennis emphatically; "they are usually dangerous, and seldom half as innocent as they look."

"But what makes you think this man is only pretending to look like a dreaming, unobservant idiot, and why do you call him American so definitely?"

"He may or may not be American; but we have to give him a name for purposes of classification," Dennis explained. "In any case his overcoat was made in the States; the cut of the lapels is quite unmistakable. I knew an American who tried everywhere to get a coat cut like that over here, and failed. As to his being observant, you seem to have overlooked one important fact. There the man stands, apparently half asleep. Occasionally he displays a certain amount of life—tucks his papers more tightly under his arms, and so on. Now, the man who has been dreaming on a station platform and is obviously going by the train would wake up to look at the clock, or glance round to see how many are travelling, and generally take an interest in the bustle of the station. But this man doesn't. Why? Because he only wakes up when his interest wanders, and that is only when he has seen all he wants to see for the moment. When we pass him the second time he will probably appear to be more awake, unless there is someone else passing him in the other direction, simply because he has seen us and sized us up and dismissed us as of no interest; or, more likely, stowed us away in his capacious memory, and, having no further use for us, he forgets to appear disinterested."

"Good Lord, Dennis!" I exclaimed, "I'd no idea you ever noticed things so keenly. What do you think he is—a detective?"

"Either that or a criminal. They are the same type of mind. One is positive and the other negative, that's all. We'll turn back and test him as we pass him. Talk golf, or fishing, or something."

So we commenced a half-hearted conversation on trout flies, and as we approached "the American" I was explaining the deadly nature of the Red Palmer after a spate and the advisability of including Greenwell's Glory on the same cast. Unfortunately, as we passed our man there were three other people coming towards us, and he was gazing over the top of the carriage with the same dreaming look that had, according to Dennis, deceived me before. But we were hardly abreast of him when his stick shot up in front of us. His arm never moved at all; it was done with a quick jerk of the wrist.

"You've dropped a paper, sir," he said to Dennis, to my utter astonishment, for I had seen no paper dropped. Dennis turned quickly, and picked up a letter which was lying on the platform behind him.

"I'm very much obliged, sir; thank you," said Dennis, as he put the letter in his pocket.

"I never saw you drop that," I exclaimed when we were safely out of earshot. "Did you?"

"There you are," my friend cried triumphantly. "You were walking beside me and you didn't spot it, and he was some distance away and he did; and you say he was half asleep."

"I say, Den," I exclaimed, laughing, "d'you think it's going to be safe to travel on this train? I wonder where he's going?"

Then we dismissed the man from our minds. The train was going in six minutes, and I joined the crowd round the rug and pillow barrow, and

prepared to make myself comfortable. Leaving
everything to the last minute, as most travellers do,
we had a hurried stirrup-cup in view of the fact that
I was about to "gang awa'," and as the train glided
out of the station Dennis turned to wire for my
breakfast-basket at Crianlarich. The one thing that
it is important to do when travelling on the West
Highland Railway I had forgotten! We had not
passed Potter's Bar before I decided that it would be
impossible to sleep, so I ferreted out the attendant
and bribed him to put me into a first-class carriage.
Better still, he showed me into a sleeper. I was dog-
tired, and in ten minutes fell fast asleep. I awoke for
a moment or two as the train snorted into a station
and drew up. I dozed again for some time, and then
the door of my sleeper opened and who should look
in but "the American."

"Say, I beg your pardon," he exclaimed
apologetically. "My mistake."

"Not at all," I replied. "Where are we now?" For
the train was still standing.

"Edinburgh," he answered. "Just leaving. Sorry to
disturb you."

I again assured him that there was no harm
done, and he turned and left me, the tassels of his
Jaeger dressing-gown trailing after him. Then I fell
asleep again, and woke up as we left Whistlefield. I
had finished my wretched ablutions—for an early
morning wash on a train is always a wretched
business—as we reached Crianlarich. I was not long
in claiming my breakfast; and when the passengers
in the refreshment-room had finished their coffee—
which seems to be the time when the train is due to
leave, and not *vice-versa*, as might be expected—the

guard was standing on the platform, flag in hand, on the point of blowing his whistle. Suddenly the head of the American shot out of the window of his carriage—no other expression describes it.

"Say, conductor," he exclaimed angrily, "where's my breakfast?"

Surely Dennis had been right about the nationality.

"What name might it be, sir?" asked the guard.

"Hilderman—J. G. Hilderman. Ordered by telegraph."

"I'll see, sir," said the guard, dashing into the refreshment-room. It did not seem to matter when the train started; but, after a further heated argument, in which the official refused to wait while a couple of eggs were being fried, Mr. Hilderman was supplied with a pot of coffee, some cold ham, and dried toast, and we recommenced our belated journey. I reached Fort William and changed on to the Mallaig train, as did Mr. Hilderman, on whom, after the breakfast episode, I had begun to look with an affectionate and admiring regard. The man who can keep a train waiting in Great Britain while the guard gets him his breakfast must be very human after all. Most of the way on the beautiful journey through Lochaber I leaned with my head out of the window, drinking in the gorgeous air and admiring the luxurious scenery of the mountain side. But, in view of the hilly nature of the track and the quality of the coal employed, it is always a dangerous adventure on the West Highland Railway, and presently I found myself with a big cinder in my eye. I was trying to remove the cause of my discomfort, and at the same time swearing softly, I am afraid, when Hilderman came up.

"I guess I'm just the man you're looking for," he said. "Show me."

In less time than it takes to tell the offending cinder was removed, and I was amazed at the delicacy and certainty of his touch. I thanked him profusely, and indeed I was really grateful to him. Naturally enough, we fell into conversation—the easy, broad conversation of two men who have never seen each other before and expect never to see each other again, but are quite willing to be friends in the meantime.

"Terrible news, this," he said presently, pulling a copy of the *Glasgow Herald* from his pocket. "I suppose you got it at Fort William?"

"No," I said. "I didn't leave the train. I wasn't thinking of newspapers. What is it?"

"A state of war exists between Great Britain and Germany as from twelve o'clock last night."

"Ah!" said I. "It has come, then." And I was surprised that I had forgotten all about the war, which was actually the cause of my presence there. I noticed with some curiosity that Hilderman looked out of the window with a strangely tense air, his lips firmly pressed together, his eyes wide open and staring. He was certainly awake now. But in a moment he turned to me with a charming smile.

"You know, I'm an American," he said. "But this hits me—hits me hard. There's a calm and peaceful, friendly hospitality about this island of yours that I like—like a lot. My own country reminds me too much of my own struggles for existence. For nearly forty years I fought for breath in America, and, but that I like now and again to run over and have a look round, you can keep the place as far as I'm concerned. I've been about here now for a good many years—not just this part, for this is nearly new to me, but about the country—and I feel that this is my quarrel, and I should like to have a hand in it."

"Perhaps America may join in yet," I suggested.

"Not she," he cried, with a laugh. "America! Not on your life. Why, she's afraid of civil war. She don't know which of her own citizens are her friends and which ain't. She's tied hand and foot. She can't even turn round long enough to whip Mexico. Don't you ever expect America to join in anything except family prayer, my boy. That's safe. You know where you are, and it don't matter if you don't agree about the wording of a psalm. If an American was told off to shoot a German, he'd ten to one turn round and say: 'Here, hold on a minute; that's my uncle!'"

"You think all the Germans in the States prefer their fatherland to their adopted country, or are they most of them spies?"

"Spies?" said Hilderman, "I don't believe in spies. It stands to reason there can't be much spying done in any country. Over here, for instance, for every German policeman in this country—for that's all a spy can be—there are about a thousand British policemen. What chance has the spy? You don't seriously believe in them, do you?" he added, smiling, as he offered me a Corona cigar.

"I don't know," I said doubtfully. I didn't want to argue with my good Samaritan. "There is no doubt a certain amount of spying done; but, of course, our policemen are hardly trained to cope with it. I daresay the whole business is very greatly exaggerated."

"You bet it is, my boy," he replied emphatically. "Going far?" he asked, suddenly changing the subject.

"North of Loch Hourn," I answered.

"Oh!" said Hilderman, with renewed interest. "Glenelg?"

"I take the boat to Glenelg and then drive back," I explained. I was in a mood to tell him just where I was going, and why, and all about myself; but I recollected, with an effort, that I was talking to a total stranger.

"Drive back?" he repeated after me, with a sudden return to his dreamy manner. Then, just as suddenly, he woke up again. "Where are we now?" he asked.

"Passing over Morar bridge," I explained.

"Dear me—yes, of course!" he exclaimed, with a glance out of the window. "Well, I must pack up my wraps. Good-bye, Mr. Ewart; I'm so glad to have met you. Your country's at war, and you look to me a very likely young man to do your best. Well, good-bye and good luck. I only wish I could join you."

"I wish you could," I replied heartily. "I shall certainly do my best. And many thanks for your kind assistance."

And so we parted, and returned to our respective compartments to put our things together; for our journey—the rail part of it, at any rate—was nearly over. And it was not until long afterwards that I realised that he had called me by my name, and I had never told him what it was.

CHAPTER III. MAINLY ABOUT MYRA

The train slowed down into Mallaig station. I thrilled with anticipation, for now I had only the journey on the boat, and Myra would be waiting for me at Glenelg. The train had hardly stopped when I seized my bag and jumped out on to the platform. The next instant I was nearly knocked back into the carriage again. A magnificent Great Dane had jumped at me with a deep bark of flattering welcome, and planted his paws on my shoulders.

"Sholto, my dear old man!" I cried in excitement, dropping my bag and looking round expectantly. It was Myra's dog, and there, sure enough, was a beautiful vision of brown eyes and brown-gold hair, in a heather-coloured Burberry costume, running down the platform to meet me.

"Well—darling?" I said, as I met her half-way.

"Well?" she whispered, as she took my hand, and I looked into the depths of those wonderful eyes. Truly I was a lucky dog. The world was a most excellent place, full of delightful people; and even if I were an impecunious young barrister I was richer than Croesus in the possession of those beautiful brown eyes, which looked on all the world with the gentle affection of a tender and indulgent sister, but which looked on me with——Oh! hang it all!—a fellow can't write about these sort of things when they affect him personally. Besides, they belong to me—thank God!

"I got your telegram, dear," said Myra, as we strolled out of the station behind the porter who had appropriated my bag. Sholto brought up the rear. He had too great an opinion of his own position to be jealous of me—or at any rate he was too dignified to show it—and he had always admitted me into the inner circle of his friendship in a manner that was very charming, if not a little condescending.

"Did you, darling?" I said, in reply to Myra's remark.

"Yes; it was delivered first thing this morning, and father was very pleased about it."

"Really!" I exclaimed. "I *am* glad. I was afraid he might be rather annoyed."

"I was a little bit surprised myself," she confessed, "though I'm sure I don't know why I should be. Dad's a perfect dear—he always was and he always will be. But he has been very determined about our engagement. When I told him you'd wired you were coming he was tremendously pleased. He kept on saying, 'I'm glad; that's good news, little woman, very good news. 'Pon my soul I'm doocid glad!' He said you were a splendid fellow—I can't think what made him imagine that—but he said it several times, so I suppose he had some reason for it. I was frightfully pleased. I like you to be a splendid fellow, Ron!"

I was very glad to hear that the old General was really pleased to hear of my visit. I had intended to stay at the Glenelg Hotel, as I could hardly invite myself to Invermalluch Lodge, even though I had known the old man all my life. Accordingly I took it as a definite sign that his opposition was wearing down when Myra told me I was expected at the house.

"And he said," she continued, "that he never heard such ridiculous nonsense as your saying you were coming to the hotel, and that if you preferred a common inn to the house that had been good enough for him and his fathers before him, you could stop away altogether. So there!"

"Good—that's great!" I said enthusiastically. "But did you come over by the boat from Glenelg, or what?"

"No, dear; I came in the motor-boat, so we don't need to hang about the pier here. We can either go straight home or wait a bit, whichever you like. I wanted to meet you, and I thought you'd rather come back with me in the motor-boat than jolt about in the stuffy old *Sheila*."

"Rather, dear; I should say I would," said I—and a lot more besides, which has nothing to do with the story. Suddenly Myra's motherly instinct awoke.

"Have you had breakfast?" she asked.

"Yes, dear—at Crianlarich. The only decent meal to be got on a railway in this country is a Crianlarich breakfast."

"Well, in that case you're ready for lunch. It's gone twelve. I could do with something myself, incidentally, and I want to talk to you before we start for home. Let's have lunch here."

I readily agreed, and after calling Sholto, who was being conducted on a tour of inspection by the parson's dog, we strolled up the hill to the hotel. As we entered the long dining-room we came upon Hilderman, seated at one of the tables with his back to us.

"Yes," he was saying to the waiter, "I have been spending the week-end on the Clyde in a yacht. I joined the train at Ardlui this morning, and I can tell you——"

I didn't wait to hear any more. Rather by instinct than as a result of any definite train of thought, I led Myra quickly behind a Japanese screen to a small table by a side window. After all, it was no business of mine if Hilderman wished to say he had joined the train at Ardlui. He probably had his own reasons. Possibly Dennis was right, and the man was a detective. But I had seen him at King's Cross and again at Edinburgh before we reached Ardlui, so I thought it might embarrass him if I walked in on the top of his assertion that he had just come from the Clyde. However, Myra was with me, which was much more important, and I dismissed Hilderman and his little fib from my mind.

"Ronnie," said Myra, in the middle of lunch, "you haven't said anything about the war."

"No, dear," I answered clumsily. "It——" It was an astonishingly difficult thing to say when it came to saying it.

"And yet that was what you came to see me about?"

"Yes, darling. You see, I——"

"I know, dear. You've come to tell me that you're going to enlist. I'm glad, Ronnie, very glad—and very, very proud."

Myra turned away and looked out of the window.

"I hate people who talk a lot about their duty," I said; "but it obviously is my duty, and I know that's what you would want me to do."

"Of course, dear, I wouldn't have you do anything else." And she turned and smiled at me, though there were tears in her dear eyes. "And I shall try to be brave, very brave, Ronnie. I'm getting a big girl now," she added pluckily, attempting a little laugh. And though, of course, we afterwards discussed the regiment I was to join, and how the uniform would suit me, and how you kept your buttons clean, and a thousand other things, that was the last that was said about it from that point of view. There are some people who never need to say certain things—or at any rate there are some things that never need be said between certain people.

After lunch we strolled round the "fish-table," a sort of subsidiary pier on which the fish are auctioned, and listened to the excited conversations of the fish-curers, gutters, and fishermen. It was a veritable babel—the mournful intonation of the East Coast, the broad guttural of the Broomielaw, mingled with the shrill Gaelic scream of the Highlands, and the occasional twang of the cockney tourist. Having retrieved Sholto, who was inspecting some fish which had been laid out to dry in the middle of the village street, and packed him safely in the bows, we set out to sea, Myra at the engine, while I took the tiller. As we glided out of the harbour I turned round, impelled by some unknown instinct. The parson's dog was standing at the head of the main pier, seeing us safely off the premises, and beside him was the tall figure of my friend J. G. Hilderman. As I looked up at him I wondered if he recognised me; but it was evident he did, for he raised his cap and waved to me. I returned the compliment as well as I could, for just then Myra turned and implored me not to run into the lighthouse.

"Someone you know?" she asked, as I righted our course.

"Only a chap I met on the train," I explained.

"It looks like the tenant of Glasnabinnie, but I couldn't be certain. I've never met him, and I've only seen him once."

"Glasnabinnie!" I exclaimed, with a new interest. "Really! Why, that's quite close to you, surely?"

"Just the other side of the loch, directly opposite us. A good swimmer could swim across, but a motor would take days to go round. So we're really a long way off, and unless he turns up at some local function we're not likely to meet him. He's said to be an American millionaire; but then every American in these parts is supposed to have at least one million of money."

"Do you know anything about him—what he does, or did?" I asked.

"Absolutely nothing," she replied, "except, of course, the silly rumours that one always hears about strangers. He took Glasnabinnie in May—in fact, the last week of April, I believe. That rather surprised us, because it was very early for summer visitors. But he showed his good sense in doing so, as the country was looking gorgeous—Sgriol, na Ciche, and the Cuchulins under snow. I've heard (Angus McGeochan, one of our crofters, told me) he was an inventor, and had made a few odd millions out of a machine for sticking labels on canned meat. That and the fact that he is a very keen amateur photographer is the complete history of Mr. Hilderman so far as I know it. Anyway, he has a gorgeous view, hasn't he? It's nearly as good as ours."

"He has indeed," I agreed readily. "But I don't think Hilderman can be very wealthy; no fishing goes with Glasnabinnie, there's no yacht anchorage, and there's no road to motor on. How does he get about?"

"He's got a beautiful Wolseley launch," said Myra jealously, "a perfect beauty. He calls her the *Baltimore II*. She was lying alongside the *Hermione* at Mallaig when we left. Oh! look up the loch, Ron! Isn't it a wonderful view?"

And so the magnificent purple-gray summit of Sgor na Ciche, at the head of Loch Nevis, claimed our attention—(that and other matters of a personal nature)—and J. G. Hilderman went completely from our minds. Myra was a real Highlander of the West. She lived for its mountains and lochs, its rivers and burns, its magnificent coast and its fascinating animal life. She knew every little creek and inlet, every rock and shallow, every reef and current from Fort William to the Gair Loch. I have even heard it said that when she was twelve she could draw an accurate outline of Benbecula and North Uist, a feat that would be a great deal beyond the vast majority of grown-ups living on those islands themselves. As we turned to cross the head of Loch Hourn, Myra pointed out Glasnabinnie, nestling like a lump of grey lichen at the foot of the Croulin Burn. Anchored off the point was a small steam yacht, either a converted drifter or built on drifter lines.

"Our friend has visitors," said Myra, "and he's not there to receive them. How very rude! That yacht is often there. She only makes about eight knots as a rule, although she gives you the impression she could do more. You see, she's been built for strength and comfort more than for looks. She calls at Glasnabinnie in the afternoons sometimes, and is there after dark, and sails off before six." (Myra was always out of doors before six in the morning, whatever the weather.) "From which I gather," she continued, "that the owner lives some distance away and sleeps on board. She can't be continuously cruising, or she would make a longer stay sometimes."

"You seem to know the ways of yacht-owners, dear," I said. "Hullo! what is that hut on the cliff above the falls? That's new, surely."

"Oh! that beastly thing," said Myra in disgust. "That's his, too. A smoking-room and study, I believe. He had it built there because he has an uninterrupted view that sweeps the sea."

"Why 'beastly thing'?" I asked. "It's too far away to worry you, though it isn't exactly pretty, and I know you hate to see anything in the shape of a new building going up."

"Oh! it annoys me," she answered airily, "and somehow it gets on daddy's nerves. You see, it has a funny sort of window which goes all round the top of the hut. This is evidently divided into several small windows, because they swing about in the wind, and when the sun shines on them they catch the eye even at our distance. And, as I say, they get on daddy's nerves, which have not been too good the last week or two."

"Never mind," I consoled her; "he'll be all right when his friends come up for the Twelfth. I think the doctors are wrong to say that he should never have a

lot of people hanging round him, because there can
surely be no harm in letting him see a few friends. I
certainly think he's right to make an exception for
the grouse."

"Grouse!" sniffed Myra. "They come for the
Twelfth because they like to be seen travelling north
on the eleventh! And I have to entertain them. And
some of the ones who come for the first time tell me
they suppose I know all the pretty walks round
about! And in any case," she finished, in high
indignation, "can you imagine *me* entertaining
anybody?"

"Yes, my dear, I can," I replied; and the
"argument" kept us busy till we reached
Invermalluch. The old General came down to the
landing-stage to meet us, and was much more
honestly pleased to see me than I had ever known
him before.

"Ah! Ronald, my boy!" he exclaimed heartily.
"'Pon my soul, I'm glad to see you. It's true, I
suppose? You've heard the news?"

The question amused me, because it was so
typical of the old fellow. Here had I come from
London, where the Cabinet was sitting night and
day, to a spot miles from the railway terminus, to be
asked if I had heard the news!

"You mean the war, of course?" I replied.

"Yes; it's come, my boy, at last. Come to find me
on the shelf! Ah, well! It had to come sooner or later,
and now we're not ready. Ah, well, we must all do
what we can. Begad, I'm glad to see you, my boy,
thundering glad. It's a bit lonely here sometimes for
the little woman, you know; but she never
complains." (In point of fact, she even contrived to

laugh, and take her father's arm affectionately in her's.) "And besides, there are many things I want to have a talk with you about, Ronald—many things. By the way, had lunch?"

"We lunched at Mallaig, thank you, sir," I explained.

"Well, well, Myra will see you get all you want—won't you, girlie?" he said.

"I say, Ronnie," Myra asked, as we reached the house, "are you very tired after your journey, or shall we have a cup of tea and then take our rods for an hour or so?"

I stoutly declared I was not the least tired—as who could have been in the circumstances?—and I should enjoy an hour's fishing with Myra immensely. So I ran upstairs and had a bath, and changed, and came down to find the General waiting for me. Myra had disappeared into the kitchen regions to give first-aid to a bare-legged crofter laddie who had cut his foot on a broken bottle.

"Well, my boy," said the old man, "you've come to tell us something. What is it?"

"Oh!" I replied, as lightly as I could, "it is simply that we are in for a row with Germany, and I've got a part in the play, so to speak. I'm enlisting."

"Good boy," he chuckled, "good boy! Applying for a commission, I suppose—man of your class and education, and all that—eh?"

"Oh, heavens, no!" I laughed. "I shall just walk on with the crowd, to continue the simile."

"Glad to hear it, my boy—I am, indeed. 'Pon my soul, you're a good lad, you know—quite a good lad. Your father would have been proud of you. He was a splendid fellow—a thundering splendid fellow. We always used to say, 'You can always trust Ewart to do the straight, clean thing; he's a gentleman.' I hope your comrades will say the same of you, my boy."

"By the way, sir," I added, "I also intended to tell you that in the circumstances I—I——Well, I mean to say that I shan't—shan't expect Myra to consider herself under—under any obligations to me."

However difficult it was for me to say it, I had been quite certain that the old General would think it was the right thing to say, and would be genuinely grateful to me for saying it off my own bat without any prompting from him. So I was quite unprepared for the outburst that followed.

"You silly young fellow!" he cried. "'Pon my soul, you are a silly young chap, you know. D'you mean to tell me you came here intending to tell my little girl to forget all about you just when you are going off to fight for your country, and may never come back? You mean to run away and leave her alone with an old crock of a father? You know, Ewart, you—you make me angry at times."

"I'm very sorry, sir," I apologised, though I had no recollection of having made him angry before.

"Oh! I know," he said, in a calmer tone. "Felt it was your duty, and all that—eh? I know. But, you see, it's not your duty at all. No. Now, there are one or two things I want to tell you that you don't know, and I'll tell you one of 'em now and the rest later. The first thing—in absolute confidence, of course—is that——"

But at this point Myra walked in, and the General broke off into an incoherent mutter. He was a poor diplomatist.

"Ah! secrets? Naughty!" she exclaimed laughingly. "Are you ready, Ronnie?"

"He's quite ready, my dear," said the old man graciously. "I've said all I want to say to him for the time being. Run along with girlie, Ewart. You don't want to mess about with an old crock."

"Daddy," said Myra reproachfully, "you're not to call yourself names."

"All right, then; I won't," he laughed. "You young people will excuse me, I'm sure. I should like to join you; but I have a lot of letters to write, and I daresay you'd rather be by yourselves. Eh?—you young dog!"

It was a polite fiction between father and daughter that when the old fellow felt too unwell to join her or his guests he "had a lot of letters to write." And occasionally, when he was in the mood to overtax his strength, she would never refer to it directly, but often she would remark, "You know you'll miss the post, daddy." And they both understood. So we set out by ourselves, and I naturally preferred to be alone with Myra, much as I liked her father. We went out on to the verandah, and while I unpacked my kit Myra rewound her line, which had been drying on the pegs overnight.

"Are you content with small mercies, Ron?" she asked, "or do you agree that it is better to try for a salmon than catch a trout?"

"It certainly isn't better to-day, anyway," I answered. "I want to be near you, darling. I don't want the distance of the pools between us. We might walk up to the Dead Man's Pool, and then fish up stream; and later fish the loch from the boat. That would bring us back in nice time for dinner."

"Oh! splendid!" she cried; and we fished out our fly-books. Her's was a big book of tattered pig-skin, which reclined at the bottom of the capacious "poacher's pocket" in her jacket. The fly-book was an old favourite—she wouldn't have parted with it for worlds. Having followed her advice, and changed the Orange I had tied for the "bob" to a Peacock Zulu, which I borrowed from her, we set out.

"Just above the Dead Man's Pool you get a beautiful view of Hilderman's hideous hut," Myra declared as we walked along. I may explain here that "Dead Man's Pool" is an English translation of the Gaelic name, which I dare not inflict on the reader.

"See?" she cried, as we climbed the rock looking down on the gorgeous salmon pool, with its cool, inviting depths and its subtle promise of sport. "Oh! Ronnie, isn't it wonderful?" she cried. "Almost every day of my life I have admired this view, and I love it more and more every time I see it. I sometimes think I'd rather give up my life than the simple power to gaze at the mountains and the sea."

"Why, look!" I exclaimed. "Is that the window you meant?"

"Yes," Myra replied, with an air of annoyance, "that's it. You can see that light when the sun shines on it, which is nearly all day, and it keeps on reminding us that we have a neighbour, although the loch is between us. Besides, for some extraordinary reason it gets on father's nerves. Poor old daddy!"

It may seem strange to the reader that anyone should take notice of the sun's reflection on a window two and a quarter miles away; but it must be remembered that all her life Myra had been accustomed to the undisputed possession of an unbroken view.

"Anyhow," she added, as she turned away, "we came here to fish. One of us must cross the stream here and fish that side. We can't cross higher up, there's too much water, and there's no point in getting wet. I'll go, and you fish this side; and when we reach the loch we'll get into the boat. See, Sholto's across already."

And she tripped lightly from boulder to boulder across the top of the fall which steams into the Dead Man's Pool, while I stood and admired her agile sureness of foot as one admires the graceful movements of a beautiful young roe. Sholto was pawing about in a tiny backwater, and trying to swallow the bubbles he made, until he saw his beloved mistress was intent on the serious business of fishing, and then he climbed lazily to the top of a rock, where he could keep a watchful eye on her, and sprawled himself out in the sun. I have fished better water than the Malluch river, certainly, and killed bigger fish in other lochs than the beautiful mountain tarn above Invermalluch Lodge; but I have never had a more enjoyable day's sport than the least satisfying of my many days there.

There was a delightful informality about the sport at the Lodge. One fished in all weathers because one wanted to fish, and varied one's methods and destination according to the day. There was no sign of that hideous custom of doing the thing "properly" that the members of a stockbroker's house-party seem to enjoy—no drawing lots for reaches or pools overnight, no roping-in a gillie to add to the chance of sending a basket "south." When there was a superfluity of fish the crofters and tenants were supplied first, and then anything that was left over was sent to friends in London and elsewhere. At the end of the day's sport we went home happy and pleased with ourselves, not in the least depressed if we had drawn a blank, to jolly and delightful meals, without any formality at all. And if we were wet, there was a great drying-room off the kitchen premises where our clothes were dried by a housemaid who really understood the business. As for our tackle, we dried our own lines and pegged them under the verandah, and rewound them again in the morning, made up our own casts, and generally did everything for ourselves without a retinue of attendants. And thereby we enjoyed ourselves hugely.

Angus and Sandy, the two handy-men of the place, would carry the lunch-basket or pull the boats on the loch or stand by with the gaff or net—and what experts they are!—but the rest we did for ourselves. By the time I had got a pipe on and wetted my line, Myra was some fifty yards or so up stream making for a spot where she suspected something. She has the unerring instinct of the inveterate poacher! I cast idly once or twice, content to revel in the delight of holding a rod in my hand once more, intoxicated with the air and the scenery and the sunshine (What a good thing the fish in the west "like it bright!"), and after a few minutes a sudden jerk on my line brought me back to earth. I missed him, but he thrilled me to the serious business of the thing, and I fished on, intent on every cast.

I suppose I must have fished for about twenty minutes, but of that I have never been able to say definitely. It may possibly have been more. I only know that as I was picking my way over some boulders to enable me to cast more accurately for a big one I had risen, I heard Myra give a sharp, short cry. I turned anxiously and called to her.

I could not distinguish her at first among the great gray rocks in the river. Surely she could not have fallen in. Even had she done so, I hardly think she would have called out. She was extraordinarily sure on her feet, and, in any case, she was an expert swimmer. What could it be? Immediately following her cry came Sholto's deep bay, and then I saw her. She was standing on a tall, white, lozenge-shaped rock, that looked almost as if it had been carefully shaped in concrete. She was kneeling, and her arm was across her face. With a cry I dashed into the river, and floundered across, sometimes almost up to my neck, and ran stumbling to her in a blind agony of fear. Even as I ran her rod was carried past me, and disappeared over the fall below.

"Myra, my darling," I cried as I reached her, and took her in my arms, "what is it, dearest? For God's sake tell me—what is it?"

"Oh, Ronnie, dear," she said, "I don't know, darling. I don't understand." Her voice broke as she lifted her beautiful face to me. I looked into those wonderful eyes, and they gazed back at me with a dull, meaningless stare. She stretched out her arm to grasp my hand, and her own hand clutched aimlessly on my collar.

In a flash I realised the hideous truth.

Myra was blind!

Chapter IV. The Black Blow

"Oh, Ronnie, darling," Myra asked, in a pitiful voice that went to my heart. "What can it mean? I—I—I can't see—anything at all."

"It's the sun, darling; it will be all right in a minute or two. There, lie in my arms, dear, and close your poor eyes. It will be all right soon, dearest."

I tried to comfort her, to assure her that it was just the glare on the water, that she would be able to see again in a moment, but I felt the pitiful inadequacy of my empty words, and it seemed that the light had gone out of my life. I pray that I may never again witness such a harrowing sight as that of Myra, leaning her beautiful head on my shoulder, suddenly stricken blind, doing her best to pacify her dog, who was heart-broken in the instinctive knowledge of a new, swift grief which he could not understand.

I must ask the reader to spare me from describing in detail the terrible agony of the next few days, when the hideous tragedy of Myra's blindness overcame us all in its naked freshness. I cannot bring myself to speak of it even yet. I would at any time give my life to save Myra's sight, her most priceless possession. I make this as a simple statement of fact, and in no spirit of romantic arrogance, and I think I would rather die than live again the gnawing agony of those days.

I took Myra in my arms, and carried her back to
the house. Poor child; she realised almost
immediately that I was as dumbfounded as she was
herself at the terrible blow which had befallen her,
and that I had no faith in my empty assurances that
it would soon be all right again, and she would be
able to see as well as ever in an hour or two, at most.
So she at once began to comfort me! I marvelled at
her bravery, but she made me more miserable than
ever. I felt that she might have a sort of premonition
that she would never see again. As we crossed the
stream above the fall I saw again the reflected light
from Hilderman's window, and a pang shot through
me as I remembered her words on that very spot—
that she would rather die than be unable to see her
beloved mountains.

I clutched her in my arms, and held her closer to
me in dumb despair.

"Am I very heavy, Ron, dear?" she asked
presently. "If you give me your hand, dear, I could
walk. I think I could even manage without it; but, of
course, I should prefer to have your hand at any
time." She gave a natural little laugh, which almost
deceived me, and again I marvelled at her pluck. I
had known Myra since she was four, and I might
have expected that she would meet her tragic
misfortune with a smile.

"You're as light as a feather, dearest," I protested,
"and, as far as that goes, I'd rather carry you at any
time."

"I'm glad you were here when it happened, dear,"
she whispered.

"Tell me, darling, how did it happen?" I asked. "I mean, what did it seem like? Did things gradually grow duller and duller, or what?"

"No," she answered; "that was the extraordinary part of it. Quite suddenly I saw everything green for a second, and then everything went out in a green flash. It was a wonderful, liquid green, like the sea over a sand-bank. It was just a long flash, very quick and sharp, and then I found I could see nothing at all. Everything is black now, the black of an intense green. I thought I'd been struck by lightning. Wasn't it silly of me?"

"My poor, brave little woman," I murmured. "Tell me, where were you then?"

"Just where you found me, on the Chemist's Rock. I call it the Chemist's Rock because it's shaped like a cough-lozenge. I was casting from there; it makes a beautiful fishing-table. I looked up, and then—well, then it happened."

"We're just coming to the house," said Myra suddenly. "We're just going to turn on to the stable-path."

"Darling!" I cried, nearly dropping her in my excitement; "you can see already?"

"Oh, Ronnie, I'm so sorry," she said penitently. "I only knew by the smell of the peat stacks." I could not restrain a groan of disappointment, and Myra stroked my face, and murmured again, "I'm sorry, dearest."

"Will you please put me down now?" she asked. "If daddy saw you carrying me to the house he'd have a fit, and the servants would go into hysterics." So I put her tenderly on her feet, and she took my arm, and we walked slowly to the house. She could see nothing, not even in the hazy confusion of the nearly blind; yet she walked to the house with as firm a step and as natural an air as if she had nothing whatever the matter with her.

"You had better leave dad to me, Ron," she suggested. "We understand each other, and I can explain to him. You would find it difficult, and it would be painful for you both. Just tell him that I'm not feeling very well, and he'll come straight to me. Don't tell him I want to see him. Give me your arm to my den, dear."

I led her to her "den," a little room opening on to the verandah. There was a writing-table in the window covered with correspondence in neat little piles, for Myra was on all the charity committees in the county, and the rest of the room was given up to a profusion of fishing tackle, shooting gear, and books. Sholto followed us, every now and then rubbing his great head against her skirt. I left her there, and turned into the hall, where I met the General. He had heard us return.

"You're back early, my boy," he remarked.

"Yes," I said, taking out my cigarette-case to give myself an air of assurance which was utterly unknown to me. "Myra is not feeling very well. She's resting for a bit."

"Not well?" he exclaimed, in surprise. "Very unusual, very unusual indeed." And he turned straight into Myra's room without waiting for an answer to his quiet tap on the door. With a heavy heart I went upstairs to the old schoolroom, now given over to Mary McNiven, Myra's old nurse.

"Master Ronald! I *am* glad," she cried, when I accepted her invitation to "come in." Mary had boxed my ears many times in my boyhood, and the fact that we were old friends made it difficult for me to tell her my terrible news. I broke it as gently as I could, and warned her not to alarm the servants, and very soon she wiped away her tears and went downstairs to see what she could do. I went out into the fresh air for a moment to pull myself together, marvelling at the unreasoning cruelty of fate. I turned into the hall, and met the General coming out of Myra's room. He was talking to Mary and one of the housemaids.

"These things often occur," he was explaining in a very matter-of-fact voice. "They are unusual, though not unheard-of, and very distressing at the time. But I am confident that Miss Myra will be quite herself again in a day or two. Meanwhile, she had better go to bed and rest, and take care of herself while Angus fetches Doctor Whitehouse. No doubt he will give her some lotion to wash her eyes with, and it will be only a day or two before we see Miss Myra about again as usual. You must see that she has no light near her, and that she rests her eyes in every possible way. There is nothing whatever for you girls to get anxious or frightened about. I have seen this sort of thing before, though usually in the East."

The old man dismissed the maids, and went into the drawing-room, while I spent a few moments with Myra. I was delighted to see the General taking it so well, as I had even been afraid of his total collapse, so I took what comfort I could from his ready assurance that he was quite accustomed to that sort of thing. But when, some twenty minutes later, I went to look for him in the drawing-room, and found him prostrate on the sofa, his head buried in his arms, I realised whence Myra had derived her pluck. He looked up as he heard the door open, and tears were streaming down his rugged old face.

"Never mind me, Ronald," he said brokenly. "Never mind me. I shall be all right in a minute. I—I didn't expect this, but I shall be all right in a minute." I closed the door softly and left him alone.

I found Angus had harnessed the pony, and was just about to start for Glenelg to fetch Doctor Whitehouse. So I told him to tell the General that I should be better able to explain to the doctor what had happened, and, glad of the diversion, I drove in for him myself. But when he arrived he made a long and searching examination, patted Myra's head, and told her the nerve had been strained by the glare on the water, and rest was all that was needed; and, as soon as he got outside her door, he sighed and shook his head. In the library he made no bones about it, and her father and I were both grateful to him.

"It's not a bit of use my saying I know when I don't," the doctor declared emphatically. "I'm puzzled—indeed, I'm absolutely beaten. This is a thing I've not only never come across before, but I've never even read about it. This green flash, the suddenness of it, the absence of pain—she says she feels perfectly well. She could see wonderfully well up to the second it happened; no warning headaches, and nothing whatever to account for it. I have known a sudden shock to the system produce instantaneous blindness, such as a man in a very heated state diving into ice-cold water. But in this case there is nothing to go by. I can only do her harm by pretending to know what I don't know, and you know as much as I do. She must see a specialist, and the sooner the better. I would recommend Sir Gaire Olvery; that would mean taking her up to London. Mr. Herbert Garnesk is the second greatest oculist in the country; but undoubtedly Sir Gaire is first. Meanwhile I will give her a little nerve tonic; it will do her no harm, and will give her reason to think that we know how to treat her, so that it may do her good. She must wear the shade I brought her, and take care her eyes are never exposed to the light."

"The fact that you yourself can make nothing of it is for us or against us?" asked the General, in an anxious voice.

He was looking haggard and tired out.

"In what way?" queried the doctor.

"I mean that if she had—er—totally lost her—the use of her eyes—for all time, could you be certain of that or not? Or can you give us any reason to hope that the very fact of your not understanding the nature of the case points to her getting over it?"

"Ah," said the doctor, "I'm not going to be so unfair to you as to say that. I will say emphatically that she has not absolutely hopelessly lost her sight. The nerves are not dead. This green veil may be lifted, possibly, as suddenly as it fell; but I am talking to men, and I want you to understand that I can give no idea as to when that may be. I pray that it may be soon—very soon."

"I'm glad you're so straightforward about it, Whitehouse," said the old man, as he sank into a chair. "I don't need to be buoyed up by any false hopes. You can understand that it is a very terrible blow to Mr. Ewart and myself."

"I can indeed," said the doctor solemnly. "I brought her into the world, you know. It is a tragic shock to me. I'll get back now, if you'll excuse me. I have a very serious case in the village, but I'll be over first thing in the morning, and I'll bring you a small bottle of something with me. You'll need it with this anxiety."

"Nonsense, Whitehouse," declared the General stoutly. "I'm perfectly all right. There's nothing at all the matter with me. I don't need any of your begad slush."

"Now, my dear friend," said the medical man cunningly, "it's my business to look ahead. In the next few days you'll be too anxious to eat, so I'm going to bring you something that will simply stimulate your appetite and make you want to eat. It's not good for any man to go without his meals, especially when that man's getting on for sixty."

"Thank ye, my dear fellow," said the old man, more graciously. "I'm sorry to be such a boor, but I thought you meant some begad tonic." The General was getting on for seventy; to be exact, he was sixty-nine—he married at forty-six—and when the medicine came he took it, "because, after all, it was begad decent of Whitehouse to have thought of it."

I spent a miserable night. I went to bed early, and lay awake till daybreak. The hideous nightmare of the green ray kept me awake for many nights to come. The General agreed with me that we must waste no time, and it was arranged that we should take Myra up to London the next day.

"You know, Ronald," said the old man to me as we sat together after the mockery that would otherwise have been an excellent dinner, "I was particularly glad to see you to-day. I've been very worried about—well, about myself lately. I had an extraordinary experience the other day which I should never dare to relate to anyone whom I could not absolutely rely on to believe me. I've been fidgeting for the last month or two, and that window that you say you saw to-day has got very much on my nerves. I've been imagining that it's a heliograph from an enemy encampment. Simply nerves, of course; but nerves ought not to account for extraordinary optical delusions or hallucinations."

"Hallucinations?" I asked anxiously. "What sort of hallucinations?"

"I hardly like to tell you, my boy," he answered, nervously twirling his liqueur glass in his fingers. "You see, you're young, and I'm—well, to tell you the truth, I'm getting old, and when you get old you get nerves, and they can be terrible things, nerves." I looked up at the haggard face, drawn into deep furrows with the new trouble that had fallen on the old man, and I was shocked and startled to see a look of absolute fear in his eyes. I leaned forward, and laid my hand on his wrist.

"Tell me," I suggested, as gently as I could. He brightened at once, and patted my arm affectionately.

"I couldn't tell the little woman," he muttered. "She—she'd have been frightened, and she might have thought I was going mad. I couldn't bear that. I hadn't the courage to tell Whitehouse either; but you're a good chap, Ronald, and you're very fond of my girlie, and your father and I were pals, as you boys would say. I daresay it was only a sort of waking dream, or——" He broke off and stared at the table-cloth. I took the glass from his hand, and filled it with liqueur brandy, and put it beside him.

He sipped it thoughtfully. Suddenly he turned to me, and brought his hand down on the table with a bang.

"I swear I'm not mad, Ronald!" he cried fiercely. "There must be some explanation of it. I know I'm sane."

"What was it exactly?" I asked quietly. "Nothing on God's earth will persuade me that you are mad, sir."

"Thank you, my boy. I'll tell you what happened to me. You won't be able to explain it, but you shall hear just what it was. You may think it's silly of me to get nervous of what sounds like an absurdity, but you see it happened where—where to-day's tragedy happened."

"What Myra calls the Chemist's Rock?" I asked, by this time intensely interested.

"At the Chemist's Rock," he replied. "It was a lovely afternoon, just such an afternoon as to-day. I had been going to fish with girlie, but I was a little tired, and—er—I had some letters to write, so I said I would meet her later in the afternoon. It was agreed we should meet at the Chemist's Rock at half-past four. I left the house about a quarter-past, and strolled down the river to the Fank Pool, crossed the stream in the boat that lies there, and walked up the opposite bank past Dead Man's Pool towards the Chemist's Rock. I mention all this to show you that I was feeling well enough to enjoy a stroll, and a very rocky stroll at that, because, if I hadn't been feeling perfectly fit, I should have gone up the back way past the stable, the way you came back this afternoon. So you see, I was undoubtedly quite well, my boy. However, to get on with the tale. As soon as I came in sight of our meeting-place I looked up to see if girlie had got there before me. She was not there. I looked further up stream, and saw Sholto come tearing down over the rocks. I knew that he had seen me, and that she was following him. I naturally strolled on to go to the rock—I say I went——" He broke off, and passed his hands across his eyes.

"Yes," I said softly; "you went to the rock, and Myra met you——"

"No," he said; "I didn't. I didn't go to the rock."

"But I don't understand," I said, as he remained silent for some moments. The old man leaned forward, and laid a trembling, fever-scorched hand on mine.

"Ronald," he said, in a voice that shook with genuine horror, and sent a cold shiver down my spine, "I did not go to the rock. *The rock came to me.*"

Chapter V. Is More Mysterious

I sat and stared at the old man in astonishment. Obviously he was fully convinced that he was giving me an accurate account of what had happened, and equally obviously he was perfectly sane.

"That is all," he said presently. "The rock came to me."

"Good heavens!" I exclaimed, suddenly brought to my senses by the sound of his voice. "What an extraordinary thing!"

"For a moment I thought I was mad, and sometimes, when I have thought over it since—and the Lord knows how many times I've done that—I've come to the conclusion that I must have fallen asleep. But even now the fear haunts me that my mind may be going."

"You mustn't imagine anything like that, General," I advised seriously. "Whatever you do, don't encourage any doubts of your own sanity. There must be some explanation of this, although I can't for the moment imagine what it can possibly be. It is a remarkable thing, and I fancy you will find, when we do know the explanation, that anyone else standing where you were at that time would have seen exactly the same thing. The rock stands out of the water; it is just above a deep pool, and probably it was a sort of mirage effect, and not by any means a figment of your brain."

To my surprise the old man leaned back in his chair and burst out laughing.

"Of course," he exclaimed. "I never thought of that—a sort of mirage. Well, I'm begad thankful you suggested that, Ronald. I've no doubt that it was something of the sort. What a begad old fool I am. Let us pray that our poor little girl's trouble," he added solemnly, "will have some equally simple solution."

The General was so relieved that I had given him, at any rate, some sort of reason to believe that his brain was not yet going, that he began to declare that he was convinced Myra would be better in a day or two. So we arranged that I should take her up to London the next day, and leave her in charge of her aunt, Lady Ruslit, and then, as soon as we had heard Sir Gaire's verdict, I was to bring her back again. General McLeod had been anxious at first to come with us, but I pointed out that he would be of more use to Myra if he stayed behind, and kept an eye on her interests in the neighbourhood. I promised to wire him the result of the interview with Olvery as soon as I knew it. And just about a quarter to ten we went to bed.

"Ronald," said the old man, as we shook hands outside my door, "there's just one thing I wasn't frank with you about in the matter of the Chemist's Rock. I am anxious to believe that it's a point of no particular importance. You know the rock is a sort of sandstone, not grey like the rest, but nearly white?"

"Yes," I answered, wondering what could be coming next.

"Well," said the old man, "that day when I saw it appearing to come towards me it was not white, but green."

"No," I said at last, when we had spent another twenty minutes discussing this new aspect in my room. "It's beyond me. I can't see how the two events can be connected, and yet they are so unusual that one would think they must be. I certainly think it is a point to put in detail before Olvery."

"On the whole, I quite agree with you," said the General. "I am rather afraid he may take us for a pack of lunatics, and refuse to be bothered with the case."

"I'm sure he won't do that," I asserted confidently. "And he may have some medical knowledge that will just shake the puzzle into place, and explain the whole mystery to us. It seems to me a most remarkable thing that these two strange affairs should have happened in exactly the same place. That it is some strange freak of nature I have no doubt, but I am absolutely at a loss to think what it can be."

It can hardly be wondered at that, as I have said before, sleep and I were strangers that night, and I was glad enough when the time came for me to get up.

Myra came down after breakfast, wonderfully brave and bright, but there was no sign whatever of her sight returning to her. The leave-taking was a wretched business, and I cannot dwell on it. Sandy started early to sail to Mallaig with the luggage, and we followed in the motor-boat, Angus at the engine, old Mary McNiven in the bows, while I took the tiller, and Myra lay on a pile of cushions at my feet, her head resting on my knee, her arm round Sholto's neck; for she had wanted the dog to see her off at the station. The old General managed to keep up a

cheery manner as he said good-bye at the landing-
stage, but he was looking so care-worn and haggard
that I was glad that he had been persuaded not to
come up to London with us. He was certainly not in a
fit state for the fatigues of a long journey. As we
passed Glasnabinnie the *Baltimore* slid out from the
side of the shed that stood on the edge of the
miniature harbour which Nature had thoughtfully
bestowed on the place.

"I can hear a motor-boat," said Myra, suddenly
sitting up.

"Yes," I replied. "It's Hilderman's."

"Is she ahead of us?" she asked.

I looked round, and saw that the *Baltimore* was
putting out to round the point.

"No, she's about level," I answered. "She's
evidently making for Mallaig. We are, if anything, a
little ahead, but they will soon pass us, I should
think."

"Oh, Ron," cried Myra, with childish excitement,
"don't let them beat us. Angus, put some life into
her. We *must* make the harbour first."

Angus did his best, and I set her course as near
in shore as I dared on that treacherous coast. The
Baltimore glided out to sea with the easy grace of a
powerful and beautiful animal, and as we passed the
jagged promontory she was coming up about thirty
yards behind us.

"Challenge him, Ron," Myra exclaimed; "you've
met him."

I turned, and saw Hilderman and two other men
in the boat, one a friend apparently, and the other
the mechanic. I stood up and waved to him.

"We'll race you to Mallaig," I shouted.

"It's a bet," he agreed readily, at the top of his voice, waving back.

It was a ding-dong business across the mouth of Nevis, and the *Baltimore* was leading, if anything, but we had not far to go, and our opponents had taken a course a good deal farther out to sea than we were. Coming up by the lighthouse, however, the *Baltimore* drew in at a magnificent pace, and swept in to pass inside the lighthouse rock. Hilderman, who was quite distinct at the short distance, stood up in the stern of the *Baltimore*, and looked at us. We were making good time, but we had no chance of outdistancing his powerful boat. But, as he looked at us, and was evidently about to shout some triumphant greeting, I saw him catch sight of Myra, lying at my feet, her face hidden in the shade over her eyes. Suddenly, without the slightest warning, he swung the tiller, and, turning out again, took the long course round the lighthouse, and we slid alongside the fish-table a good minute ahead of him. Myra was delighted; she had no suspicion that we had virtually lost the race, and the trifling excitement gave her a real pleasure. Angus, I could see, was puzzled, but I signed to him to say nothing. My heart warmed to Hilderman; he had seen that Myra was not well, and, divining that it would give her some pleasure to win the race, he had tactfully given way to us. I was really grateful to him for his kindly thought, and determined to thank him as soon as I could. We had nearly half an hour to wait for the mid-day train, and, after seeing Myra and Mary safely ensconced in the Marine Hotel, I went out with Sholto to get the tickets, telegraph to Dennis, and express my gratitude to Hilderman. But when I stepped out of the hotel he was standing in the road waiting for me.

"Good morning, Mr. Ewart," he said, coming forward to offer me his hand. "Is there anything the matter with Miss McLeod?"

"She's not very well," I replied. "She has something the matter with her eyes. It was very good of you to let us win our little race. Every little pleasure that we can give Miss McLeod just at this time is of great value to us."

"Eyes?" said Hilderman, thoughtfully, with the same dreamy expression that Dennis had pointed out at King's Cross. "What sort of thing is it? I know something about eyes."

"I'm afraid I can tell you nothing," I replied. "She has suddenly lost her sight in the most amazing and terrible manner. We are just taking her up to London to see a specialist."

"Had she any pain?" he asked, "or any dizziness or fainting, or anything like that?"

"No," I said; "there is absolutely nothing to go by. It is a most extraordinary affair, and a very terrible blow to us all."

"It must be," he said gently, "very, very terrible. I have heard so much about Miss McLeod that I even feel it myself. I am deeply grieved to hear this, deeply grieved." He spoke very sympathetically, and I felt that it was very kind of him to take such a friendly interest in his unknown neighbour.

"I think you'd better join me in a brandy and soda, Mr. Ewart," he said, laying a hand on my arm. "I don't suppose you know it, but you look ten years older than you did yesterday."

Yesterday! Good heavens! Had all this happened in a day? I was certainly feeling far from myself, and I accepted his invitation readily enough. We turned into the refreshment-room outside the station, and I had a stiff whisky and soda, realising how far away from London I was when the man gave me the whisky in one glass and the soda in another.

"Tell me," said Hilderman, "if it is not very rude of me to ask, or too painful for you to speak about, what was Miss McLeod doing when this happened? Reading, or what?" I gave him a rough outline of the circumstances, but, in view of what the General had told me the night before, I said nothing about the mystery of the green ray. We wanted to retain our reputation for sanity as long as we could, and no outsider who did not know the General personally would believe that his astonishing experience was anything other than the strange creation of a nerve-wrought brain.

"And that was all?" he asked thoughtfully.

"Yes, that was all," I replied.

"I suppose you haven't decided what specialist you will take her to when you get her to London?" he queried. I was about to reply when I heard Sholto in a heated argument with some other dog, and I bolted out, with a hurried excuse, to bring him in. As I returned, with my hand on his collar, the harbour-master greeted me, and told me we might have some difficulty in reaching London, as the train service was likely to be disorganised owing to the transport of troops and munitions. When I rejoined Hilderman I was full of this new development. It would be both awkward and unpleasant to be turned out of the train before we reached London; and every moment's delay might mean injury to my poor Myra.

"I don't think you need worry at all, Mr. Ewart," my new friend assured me. "The trains will run all right. They may alter the services where they have too many trains, but here they are not likely to do so. Thank heaven, I shall not be travelling again for some time. I hate it, although I have to run about a good deal. I have a few modest investments that take up a considerable portion of my time. I figure on one or two boards, you know."

I thanked him for his kindly interest, and left him. I wired to Dennis not to meet the train, but to be prepared to put me up the following night. Then I got the tickets, and took Myra to the train. Hilderman was seeing his friend off; a short, somewhat stout man, with flaxen hair, and small blue eyes peering through a pair of large spectacles. He bowed to us as we passed, and I was struck by the kindly sympathy with which both he and his companion glanced at Myra. Evidently they both realised what a terrible blow to her the loss of her sight must be. I will admit that, when it came to the time for the train to start, my heart nearly failed me altogether. The sight of the beautiful blind girl saying good-bye to her dog was one which I hope I may never see again. As the train steamed out into the cutting Sholto was left whining on the platform, and it was as much as Angus could do to hold him back. Poor Sholto; he was a faithful beast, and they were taking his beloved mistress away from him. Myra sat back in the carriage, and furtively wiped away a tear from her poor sightless eyes.

"Poor old fellow," she said, with a brave smile. "If they can't do anything for me in London he will have to lead me about. It'll keep him out of mischief."

"Don't say that, darling!" I groaned.

"Poor old Ron," she said tenderly. "I believe it's worse for you than it is for me. And now that Mary has left us for a bit I want to say something to you, dear, while I can. You mustn't think I don't understand what this will mean to you, dear. I want you to know, darling, that I hope always to be your very great friend, but I don't expect you to marry a blind girl."

I shall certainly not tell the reader what I said in reply to that generous and noble statement.

"Besides, dear," I concluded eventually, "you will soon be able to see again." And so I tried to assure her, till presently Mary returned. And then we made her comfortable, and I read to her in the darkened carriage until at last my poor darling fell into a gentle sleep.

But twenty-six hours later, when I had seen Myra safely back to her aunt's house from Harley Street, I staggered up the stairs to Dennis's rooms in Panton Street a broken man.

Dennis opened the door to me himself.

"Ronald!" he cried, "what has happened?"

"Hello, old man," I said weakly; "I'm very, very tired."

My friend took my arm and led me into his sitting-room, and pressed me gently on the sofa. Then he brought me a stiff brandy and soda, and sat beside me in silence for a few minutes.

"Feel better, old boy?" he asked presently.

"Yes, thanks, Den," I answered. "I'm sorry to be such a nuisance."

"Tell me," he said, "when you feel well enough." But I lay, and closed my eyes, for I was dog-tired, and could not bring myself to speak even to Dennis of the specialist's terrible verdict. And soon Nature asserted herself, and I fell into a deep sleep, which was the best thing I could have done. When I awoke I was lying in bed, in total darkness, in Dennis's extra room. I sat up, and called out in my surprise, for I had been many miles away in my slumbers, and my first hope was that the whole adventure had been a hideous nightmare. But Dennis, hearing my shout, walked in to see if I wanted anything.

"Now, how do you feel?" he asked, as he sat on the side of the bed.

"Did you carry me in here and put me to bed?" I asked idly.

"You certainly didn't look like walking, and I thought you'd be more comfortable in here," he laughed.

"Great Scott, man!" I cried, suddenly remembering his heart trouble, "you shouldn't have done that, Dennis. You promised me you'd take no risks."

"Heavens! that was nothing," he declared emphatically. "You're as light as a feather. There was no risk in that."

Indeed, as events were to prove, it was only the first of many, but being ignorant of that at the time, I contented myself with pointing out that very few feathers turned the scale at twelve-stone-three.

"Now look here, old son," said Dennis, in an authoritative voice. "You mustn't imagine I'm dealing with your trouble, whatever it is (for you *are* in trouble, Ronald), in a matter-of-fact and unsympathetic way. But what you've got to do now is to get up, have a tub, slip into a dressing-gown, and have a quiet little dinner with me here. It's just gone eight, so you ought to be ready for it."

He disappeared to turn on the bath-water, and then, when he met me in the passage making for the bathroom, he handed me a glass.

"Drink this, old chap," he said.

"What is it?" I asked suspiciously. "I don't want any fancy pick-me-ups. They only make you worse afterwards."

"That was prescribed by Doctor Common Sense," he answered lightly. "It's peach bitters!"

After my tub I was able to tackle my dinner, with the knowledge that I was badly in need of something to eat, a feeling which surprised me very much. Throughout the meal Dennis told me of the enlistment of Jack and poor Tommy Evans, and we discussed their prospects and the chances of my seeing them before they disappeared into the crowded ranks of Kitchener's Army. Dennis himself had been ruthlessly refused. He spoke of trying his luck again until they accepted him, but I knew, from what he told me of the doctor's remarks, that he had no earthly chance of being passed. He seemed to have entirely mastered his regret at his inability to serve his country in the ranks, but I understood at once that he was merely putting his own troubles in the background in face of my own. The meal over, we "got behind" two of Dennis's excellent cigars, and made ourselves comfortable.

"Now then, old man," said my friend, "a complete and precise account of what has happened to you since you left King's Cross two days ago."

"It has all been so extraordinary and terrible," I said, "that I hardly know where to begin."

"I saw you last at the station," he said, laying a hand on my knee. "Begin from there." So I began at the beginning, and told him just what had happened, exactly as I have told the reader.

Dennis was deeply moved.

"And then you saw Olvery?" he asked. "What did he say?"

I got up, paced the room. What had Olvery said? Should I ever forget those blistering words to the day of my death?

"Come, old boy," said Dennis kindly. "You must remember that Olvery is merely a man. He is only one of the many floundering about among the mysteries of Nature, trying to throw light upon darkness. You mustn't imagine that his view is necessarily correct, from whichever point he looked at the case."

"Thank you for that," I said. "I am afraid I forgot that he might possibly be mistaken. He says he knows nothing of this case at all; he can make nothing of it; it is quite beyond him. He is certain that no such similar case has been brought to the knowledge of optical science. His view is that there is the remotest possibility that this green veil may lift, but he says he is sure that if there were any scientific reason for saying that her sight will be restored he would be able to detect it."

"I prefer your Dr. Whitehouse to this man any day," said Dennis emphatically. "He took just the opposite view. This man Olvery, like so many specialists, is evidently a dogmatic egotist."

"I'm very glad you can give us even that hope. But the eyes are such a delicate instrument. It is difficult to see how the sight can be recovered when once it has gone. Of course, Olvery is going to do what he can. He has suggested certain treatment, and massage, and so forth, and he has no objection to her going back home again. Myra, of course, is tremendously anxious for me to take her back to her father. She is worrying about him already; and, fortunately, Olvery knows Whitehouse, and has the highest opinion of him."

"Go back as soon as you can, old chap," Dennis advised. "Wire me if there is anything I can do for you at this end. I'll make some inquiries, and see if I can find out anything about any similar cases, and so on. But you take the girl back home if she wants to go."

While we were still talking, Dennis's man, Cooper, entered.

"Telegram for Mr. Ewart, sir," he said.

I took the yellow envelope and opened it carelessly.

"What is it?" cried Dennis, springing to his feet as he saw my face.

"Read it," I said faintly, as I handed it to him. Dennis read the message aloud:

"Come back at once. I can't stand this. Sholto is blind.—McLEOD."

CHAPTER VI. CONTAINS A FURTHER ENIGMA

Back again at King's Cross. I seemed to have been travelling on the line all my life. Myra turned to Dennis to say good-bye.

"I hope," she said bravely, "that when we meet again, Mr. Burnham, I shall be able to tell you that I can see you looking well."

"I do hope so, indeed, Miss McLeod," said Dennis fervently, with a quick glance at me. He was lost in admiration at the quiet calm with which my poor darling took her terrible affliction.

"Good-bye, old chap," my friend said to me cheerily. "I hope to hear in a day or two that Miss McLeod is quite well again. And," he added in a whisper, "wire me if I can be of the slightest use."

I readily agreed, and I was beginning, even at that early stage, to be very thankful that my friend was free to help me in case of need.

When at last we reached Invermalluch Lodge again I sat for an hour in the library with the old General, telling him in detail the result of the specialist's examination, but I took care to put Dennis's point of view to him at the outset. I was glad I had done so, for he seized on the faint hope it offered, and clung to it in despair.

"What is your own impression of Olvery?" he asked.

"I fancy his knighthood has got into his head," I replied. "He gave me the impression that he was quite certain he knew everything there was to be

known, and that the mere fact of his not being sure
about the return of her sight made him positive that
it must be complete and absolute blindness. Of
course he hedged and left himself a loophole in the
event of her recovery, but I could have told him just
as much as he told me."

"You say you took it on yourself to take Myra out
of his hands altogether. Why?"

"When I received your wire, I rang him up at
once, and asked him to see me immediately," I
replied. "Eventually he agreed, and I took a taxi to
his place, and told him about Sholto. He gave his
opinion without any consideration whatever. He
said: 'The merest coincidence, Mr. Ewart—the
merest coincidence—and you may even find that the
dog has not actually lost his sight at all.' So
naturally I thanked him, gave him his fee, and came
away. I propose now that you should try and get this
man—Garnish, is it——?"

"Garnesk," interposed the General, consulting a
note Dr. Whitehouse had left—"Herbert Garnesk."

"Well, I want you to try and get him sufficiently
interested to come here—and stop here—until he
has come to some decision, no matter what it is."

"A thundering good idea, Ronald," agreed the old
man. "But we can't tell him this extraordinary story
in writing."

"I'll go and find him, and fetch him back with me,
if I have to hold a gun to his head."

Accordingly I dashed off to Mallaig again, and
caught the evening train to Glasgow. I spent an
unhappy night at the Central Station Hotel—though
it was certainly not the fault of the hotel—and
looked up Mr. Garnesk as early in the morning as I

dared disturb a celebrated consultant oculist. I took a fancy to the man at once. He was young—in the early 'forties—very alert-looking, and exceedingly businesslike. His prematurely grey hair gave an added air of importance to the clever eye and clean-cut features, and he had a charm of manner which would have made his fortune had he been almost ignorant of the rudiments of his calling.

"So that's the complete story of Miss McLeod and her dog Sholto," he mused, when I had finished speaking. For a brief second I thought he was about to laugh at the apparent absurdity of the yarn, but before I had time to answer he spoke again.

"Miss McLeod and her dog are apparently blind, and Mr. Ewart is a bundle of nerves—and this is very excellent brandy, Mr. Ewart. Allow me."

I accepted the proffered glass with a laugh, in spite of myself.

"What do you think of it?" I asked.

He sat on the edge of the table and swung his leg, wrapt in thought for a moment.

"I'm very glad to say I don't know what to think of it," he replied presently.

"Why glad?" I asked anxiously.

"Because, my dear sir, this is so remarkable that if I thought I could see a solution I should probably be making a mistake. This is something I am learning about for the first time; and, frankly, it interests me intensely."

Suddenly he sat down abruptly, with a muttered "Now, then," and began to catechise me in a most extraordinarily searching manner, firing off question after question with the rapidity of a maxim gun.

I shall not detain the reader with details of this catechism. His inquiries ranged from the system on which the house was lighted and the number of hours Myra averaged per week on the sea to the make of the engine in her motor-boat. His last question was: "Does anybody drink the river water?"

"Windows that flash in the sun seem to me to be confusing the issue," he said at last. "Windows must always reflect light in a certain direction at a certain time, and though they may be irritating they could not possibly produce even temporary blindness. Still, we won't forget them, Mr. Ewart, though we had better put them aside for a moment. Now, how soon can you bring Miss McLeod to see me?"

"We had hoped," I ventured to suggest, "that you would be able to run up and see her, and have a look at the ground. You could then examine the dog as well."

"I'll be perfectly candid with you, Mr. Ewart," he replied. "I was just going to start on a short holiday. I was going to Switzerland; but the war has knocked that on the head, so I am just running up to Perthshire for a week's fishing. I need a holiday very badly, more especially as I have undertaken some Government work in connection with the war. Fortunately, I am a bachelor, and I will willingly give up a couple of days to Miss McLeod."

"Why not combine business with pleasure?" I suggested. "There's good fishing at Invermalluch, gorgeous scenery, a golf-course a mile or two away, and you can do just as you please on the General's estate. He'll be delighted."

"Are you sure?" he asked. "Well, anyway, I can go to the Glenelg Hotel and fish up Glenmore. Now, Mr.

Ewart, we will catch the afternoon train, the earliest
there is—though I suppose there's only one."

"I can't tell you how grateful I am, Mr. Garnesk,"
I said. "It may mean a very great deal to us that you
are so anxious to see Miss McLeod."

"I am not anxious to see Miss McLeod," he
answered, cryptically. "I'm anxious to see the dog."

I left him, to telegraph to the General that I was
arriving that night bringing the specialist with me;
and I need hardly say that I left the telegraph office
with a comparatively light heart. The journey to
Mallaig was one of the most interesting afternoons I
have spent. Garnesk was consulting oculist to all the
big chemical, machine, naval and other
manufacturers in the great industrial centre on the
Clyde, and he kept me enthralled with his accounts
of the sudden attacks of various eye diseases which
were occasionally the fate of the workers. The effects
of chemicals, the indigenous generation of gases in
the furnace-rooms, and so on, had afforded him
ample scope for experiment; and, fortunately for us
all, he was delighted to have found new ground for
enlarging his experience. The mixture of professional
anecdote and piscatorial prophecy with which he
entertained me, now and then rushing across the
carriage to get a glimpse of a salmon-pool in some
river over which we happened to be passing, gave me
an amusing insight into the character of one whom I
have since learned to regard as a very brilliant and
charming man. When we arrived at the landing-
stage at the Lodge, the General greeted him with
undisguised joy.

"Begad! Mr. Garnesk," he blurted, "I'm thundering glad to see you, sir. It's good of you to come, sir—extremely good."

"That remains to be seen, General," said Garnesk, solemnly—"whether my visit will do any good. I hope so, with all my heart."

"Amen to that!" said the old man, pathetically, with a heavy sigh.

"How is Miss McLeod?" asked the scientist.

"Her eyes are no better," the General replied. "She cannot see at all. Otherwise she is in perfect health. She says she feels as well as ever she did. I can't understand it," he finished helplessly.

A suit-case, a bag of golf-clubs, and a square deal box completed Garnesk's outfit.

"Steady with that—here, let me take it?" he cried, as Angus was lifting the last item ashore. "Business and pleasure," he continued, raising the box in his arms and indicating his clubs and fishing-rods with a jerk of the head. "I've one or two things here that may help me in my work, and as they are very delicate instruments I would rather carry them myself."

As we approached the house the sound of the piano greeted us in the distance; and soon we could distinguish the strains of that most beautiful and understanding of all burial marches, Grieg's "Aase's Tod."

"My daughter can even welcome us with a tune," said the old man proudly. To him all music came under the category of "tunes," with the sole exception of "God Save the King," which was a national institution.

Garnesk stopped and stood on the path, the deal box clasped carefully in his arms, his head on one side, listening.

"We have the right sort of patient to deal with, anyway," he remarked, with a sigh of relief. But to me the melancholy insistence of the exquisite harmonies was fraught with ill-omen, and I could not restrain the shudder of an unaccountable fear as we resumed our walk. Later on, when I found an opportunity to ask her why she had chosen that particular music, I was only partially relieved by her ingenuous answer:

"Oh! just because I love it, Ronnie," she said, "and there are no difficult intervals to play with your eyes shut. I thought it was rather clever of me to think of it. I shall soon be able to play more tricky things. It will cure me of looking at the notes when I can see again."

Myra and the young specialist were introduced; and, though he chatted gaily with her, and touched on innumerable subjects, he never once alluded to her misfortune. Though the General was evidently anxious that Garnesk should make his examination as soon as possible, hospitality forced him to suggest dinner first, and I was surprised at the alacrity with which the visitor concurred, knowing, as I did, his intense interest in the case. But, after a few conventional remarks to the General and Myra, I was about to show him to his room when he seized my arm excitedly.

"Quick!" he whispered. "Where's the dog?"

I led him to a room above the coach-house where poor Sholto was a pitiful prisoner. Garnesk deposited his precious packing-case on the floor, and called the dog to him. Sholto sprang forward in a moment, recognising the tone of friendship in the voice, and planted his paws on my companion's chest. For twenty minutes the examination lasted. One strange test after another was applied to the poor animal; but he was very good about it, and seemed to understand that we were trying to help him.

"I should hate to have to kill that dog, but it may be necessary before long," said the specialist. "But why didn't you tell Miss McLeod her dog was blind?"

"We were afraid it would upset her too much," I answered, and then suddenly realising the point of the question, I added, "but how on earth did you know we hadn't?"

"Because," he said thoughtfully, "if you had, she strikes me as the sort of girl who would have asked me straight away what I thought I could do for him."

"You seem to understand human nature as well as you do science," I said admiringly.

"The two are identical, or at least co-incident, Mr. Ewart," he replied solemnly. "But what was it you *did* tell her?"

"We said he was suffering from a sort of eczema, which looked as if it might be infectious, and we thought she ought not to be near him for a bit. Otherwise, of course, she would have wanted him with her all the time."

When the examination was over for the time being, I chained Sholto to a hook in an old harness-rack, for he was strong and unused to captivity, and the door had no lock, only a small bolt outside. Garnesk packed away his instruments, carried them carefully to the house, and then we sprinted upstairs to dress hurriedly for dinner.

Myra, poor child, was sensitive about joining us, but the specialist was very anxious that she should do so, and we all dined together. There was no allusion whatever to the strange events which had brought us together, but, with my professional knowledge of the mysteries of cross-examination, I noticed that Garnesk contrived to acquire more knowledge of various circumstances on which he seemed to wish to be enlightened than Sir Gaire Olvery had gleaned from forty minutes' blunt questioning.

Myra had hardly left us after the meal was over when the butler handed the General a card, and almost simultaneously a tall, shadowy figure passed the window along the verandah.

"'Pon my soul, that's kind of him," said the simple-hearted old man. "Run after him, Ronald, and fetch him back."

"Who is it?" I asked, rising.

"'Mr. J. G. Hilderman wishes to express his sympathy with General McLeod in his daughter's illness.' Very neighbourly indeed."

I ran out after Hilderman, and found that his long legs had taken him nearly half-way to the landing-stage by the time I overtook him. He stopped as I called his name.

"Why, Mr. Ewart," he exclaimed in surprise, "you back again already? I hope you had a very satisfactory interview with the specialist."

I told him briefly that our visit to London had given us no satisfaction at all, and gave him the General's invitation to come up to the house.

"I wouldn't think of it, Mr. Ewart," he declared emphatically. "Very kind of General McLeod, but he don't want to worry with strangers just now."

He was very determined; but I insisted, and he eventually gave way. I was glad he had come. I had a somewhat unreasonable esteem for his abilities and resource, and every assistance was welcomed with open arms at Invermalluch Lodge at that time. His extensive knowledge even included some slight acquaintance with the body's most wonderful organ, for he told us some very interesting eye cases he had heard of in the States. He was genuinely dumbfoundered when we told him that Sholto was an additional victim.

"You don't say so!" he exclaimed. "Well, that *is* remarkable. It sounds as if it came out of a book. In broad daylight a young lady goes out, and is as well as can be. An hour later she is stone blind. Two days afterwards her dog goes out, and *he* comes in blind. Yes, it's got me beaten."

"It's got us all beaten," said Garnesk deliberately, and I was shocked to hear him say it. I reflected that he had not even examined Myra, and my disappointment was the keener that he should admit himself nonplussed so early. But he left me no loophole of doubt.

"I can make nothing whatever of it," he added, ruefully shaking his head. "I wonder if I ever shall?"

"Come, come! my dear sir," said Hilderman cheerily. "You scientist fellows have a knack of making your difficulties a little greater than they really are, in order to get more credit for surmounting them. I know your little ways. I'm an

American, you know, professor; you can't get me that way."

Garnesk laughed—fortunately. And again I was grateful to Hilderman for his timely tact, for it cheered the old man immensely, and helped me a little, too. Presently the General left the room, and Garnesk leaned forward.

"Mr. Hilderman," he said earnestly, "do everything in your power to keep the old man's spirits up. I can give him no hope, professionally—I dare not. But you, a layman, can. It is difficult in the circumstances for Mr. Ewart to give much encouragement, but I know he will do his best."

"J. G. Hilderman is yours to command," said the American, with a bow that included us both. And then the oculist suggested that we should have a look at Sholto. I led the way to the coach-house with a heavy heart. I should not have minded a mystery which would have endangered my own life. Apart from any altruism, the personal peril would have afforded a welcome stimulant. But this unseen horror, which stabbed in the dark and robbed my beautiful Myra of her sight, chilled my very soul. I climbed wearily up the wooden stair to Sholto's new den, carrying a stable lantern in my hand, for it was getting late, and the carefully darkened room would be as black as ink. The other two followed close on my heels. I opened the door and called to the dog. A faint, sickly-sweet odour met me as I did so.

"You give your dogs elaborate kennels," said Hilderman, as he climbed the stairs, and I laughed in reply.

At that instant Garnesk stood still and sniffed the air. With a sudden jerk he wrenched the lantern from my hand and strode into the room. Sholto was gone. Only half his chain dangled from the hook, cut through the middle with a pair of strong wire-nippers.

The oculist turned to us with an expression of acute interest.

"Chloroform," he said quietly.

Chapter VII. The Chemist's Rock

By the time we gave up our hunt for Sholto that night and saw Hilderman into the *Baltimore II.* at the landing-stage, the harvest moon had splashed the mountain side with patches of silver in reckless profusion. But we were in no mood for aesthetics. We applied the moonlight to more practical purposes.

"Show me the river, Mr. Ewart," said Garnesk, as we turned away from the shore. Accordingly I took him up stream till we came to Dead Man's Pool.

"What do you make of things now?" I asked, as we walked along.

"I can't make anything of the stealing of a dog except that someone coveted it and has now got it. Can you?"

"No," I answered thoughtfully, "I can't. But it's an extraordinary coincidence, at the least; and who on earth could have stolen him? You see, no one round here would dream of taking anything that belonged to Miss McLeod. And, though Sholto is well enough bred, he's never been in a show, and has no reputation. I can't make it out."

"I'm very sorry it happened just now," said the oculist. "I was in hopes that by experimenting on the animal I could cure the girl. But at any rate that is beyond grieving about now. Is this the place?"

"Yes," I said, "this is Dead Man's Pool. That dim white shape there is the Chemist's Rock. It was there that Miss McLeod lost her sight, and here that the General had his extraordinary experience. It looks innocent and peaceful enough," I added, with a sigh.

"The General was very lucky—very lucky indeed!" murmured my companion.

"Why?" I asked.

"He was down here looking at the rock, and he saw some sort of vision; Miss McLeod was up at the rock looking down at the pool, and she lost her sight. The General might have been looking this way instead of that, in which case we might have had another case on our hands."

"Then you think the two adventures are different aspects of the same thing? If only we knew where Sholto was it might give us even more to go on."

"Have you any tobacco?" he asked abruptly. "I've got a pipe, but I left my tobacco in my room."

We were in evening dress, and my pouch and pipe were in the house; so I left him there while I ran in to fetch them. When I returned he was nowhere to be seen, and for a moment I half suspected some new tragedy; but as I looked round I caught the gleam of the moonlight on his shirt-front. I found him kneeling on the Chemist's Rock, looking out to sea.

"Many thanks, Mr. Ewart," he said, as he handed me back my pouch and took the light I offered him. "Ah! I'm glad to see you smoke real tobacco. By the way," he added, "have you a friend—a real friend—you can trust?"

"I have, thank God!" I replied fervently. "Why?"

"I should like you to send for him. Do anything you can to get him here at once. Go and drag him here, if you like—only get him here."

"But why this urgency?" I asked again. "I admit that we have some very horrible natural phenomena to deal with; but, apart from the fact that some wretched poacher has stolen a dog, we have no human element to fear. I don't see how he can help, and he might run a risk himself."

"Never mind—fetch him or send for him. If you could have seen yourself start when you returned to the pool yonder to find me missing, you would realise that your nervous system would be the better for a little congenial companionship. Frankly, Mr. Ewart, I don't like the idea of you being left alone here during the next few days with a blind girl and an old man—if you'll pardon me for being so blunt."

"But you'll be here," I said; "and I hope you will have something to say to us that will put nerves out of the question when you have examined Myra."

Garnesk rose to his feet and laid a friendly hand on my arm.

"As soon as I've seen what this place looks like at a quarter-past four to a quarter-past five in the afternoon I shall leave you."

"But—good heavens, man!" I cried, aghast, "you won't leave us like that. We hoped for so much from your visit. You can't realise, man, what it may mean to—to us all! You see——"

"My dear chap," said my companion, cutting me short with a laugh, "it is just because I do realise that my presence here may be dangerous to Miss McLeod that I propose to leave."

"Dangerous to her?" I gasped. "What on earth do you mean now?" The whole world seemed to have taken leave of its senses, and I mentally vowed that I should wire for Dennis first thing in the morning.

"I say that because her dog has been drugged and taken away."

"But some fool of a poacher was responsible for that!" I cried.

My companion looked at me thoughtfully as he puffed at his pipe.

"I was the cause of the dog's disappearance," he said quietly.

"I see what you're driving at," I said. "You pretended to steal the dog because you were afraid Myra would make overwhelming objections to your vivisecting him, or whatever you want to do. Of course, now I see you would be the only person about Invermalluch Lodge likely to have chloroform. But even then I don't see what you mean by saying that your presence here would be dangerous to Miss McLeod."

"That's a very ingenious construction to put on my words, my dear fellow," he said; "but in my mind I was relying on you to overcome my patient's objections to any experiments that might be deemed advisable on her dog. I meant something much more serious than that. I have known you only a few hours, Mr. Ewart; but nobody need tell me you are anything of a fool, unless he wants a very flat contradiction. You are looking at this affair from a personal point of view—and no wonder, either. But if you were not so worried about your *fiancee* your brain would have grasped my point at once. That is why I want you to send for a friend."

"I will," I promised solemnly. "Now tell me—what did you mean?"

"When I said I was the cause of the dog's disappearance, I meant that if I hadn't arrived on the scene the dog would never have been touched. The dog was taken by someone who knew he was blind, who knew that I would experiment on him, and who was determined to get there first."

"But," I exclaimed, "that would be carrying professional jealousy a bit too far—if that's what you mean!"

"It would be carrying it so far that we can rule it out of court," he answered. "So that's what I don't mean. Let's go back and analyse the occurrence. I say the dog was not stolen by poachers, because of the chloroform; you said the same yourself. I say that the thief knew the dog was blind, because he knew he was in a darkened room above the coach-house, and he stole him from there. A poacher would have gone to the kennel, and found it empty—and that would have been the end of that. But the man who knew the dog was in a special room must have known why he was there; and it seems to me that the man who steals a blind dog steals him because, for some reason or other, he wants a blind dog—that very one, probably. Have you got me?"

"Yes," I said, "I follow you so far. Go on." And I was surprised to find how relieved I was at this suggested complication. I felt that if we could only attribute this amazing week of mysteries to some human agent I should be able to grapple with it.

"Now I come to my main point," Garnesk continued, "and it's this: The man who wanted Sholto because he was blind wanted him to experiment on. But no professional man would do a thing like that, even supposing there to be one about. That motive again is ruled out of court. There remains one possible solution——"

"Well?" I asked breathlessly, for even now I failed to grasp the conclusion my scientific companion could be coming to. "Go on!"

"If this thief did not want Sholto to experiment on himself, he stole the dog in order to prevent me from experimenting on him."

I laughed aloud from sheer excitement and the relief of finding some tangible thing to go on, for the oculist's argument struck me as very nearly perfect.

"You ought to be at Scotland Yard," I said. "You seem to me to have hit the nail on the head."

"The two callings are very closely allied," he said modestly. "Detectives deal with murderers and thieves, and I with nerves and tissues. It is all a question of diagnosis."

"I must say I think you've diagnosed this case very well, Mr. Garnesk," I said, "though we are just at the beginning of our troubles if what you suppose is correct."

"I can't think of any other solution," he answered thoughtfully; "and we are, as you say, just at the beginning of our troubles. The first thing to do is——"

"To find the man who stole the dog," I cut in.

"To find the man who knew the dog was blind," he corrected. "By that means we may come to the man who stole the dog; then we may get his reason from his own lips, if we are exceptionally lucky. But I fancy I can supply his motive, failing a full confession."

"You can?" I cried. "Let's hear it."

"You've thought of one yourself, of course?" he asked.

"The only motive I can think of is too fantastic altogether. It is weak enough to presuppose that someone has a grievance against Miss McLeod or the General, and that someone took advantage of the extraordinary circumstances to steal Sholto, and if possible prevent Myra getting her sight back. Oh, it's too ridiculous!"

"We have to remember," my companion suggested, "that our unknown quantity not only knew that the dog was blind, but also knew that I was coming or had arrived, and would probably experiment on the beast. It argues a very terrible urgency that the animal disappeared within an hour or two of my arrival. From all that I deduce what seems to me the only possible motive. The dog was stolen by the man who made Miss McLeod blind."

"*Made* her blind!" I cried. "You don't seriously mean that you think someone—some fiend of hell—deliberately blinded her?"

"Not deliberately," my companion replied. "But I believe it was through some human agency that she was blinded. I think some person or persons were anxious that Miss McLeod should remain blind, in case we should, in the process of recovering her sight, hit upon the cause of her losing it."

In silence I sat for a few moments, thinking over this extraordinary new outlook. I must certainly wire for Dennis in the morning.

"Mr. Garnesk," I said presently, "you are bringing a very terrible charge against some human monster whom we have yet to discover. But I must admit that you seem to have logic on your side. It remains for me to discover who these people are—if there are more than one."

"Yes," he mused; "that is what we must discover."

"We!" I exclaimed. "Then you're not going away?"

"Yes," he said. "I think it would be fairer to you all if I left you. I think my arrival has done some good—my departure may do more. But I assure you, Mr. Ewart, I shall not give up this case till Miss McLeod recovers her sight. I give you my hand on that."

I shook hands with him warmly.

"Thank you," I said, as I noticed the eager look on his keen, handsome face. "Thank you from the bottom of my heart. To-morrow I hope I shall find the man who knew Sholto was blind."

"I only know of one outside the General's household," he answered.

"But I don't even know that!" I cried, forgetting Dennis for the moment. As for Olvery, he had gone clean out of my mind. "Who do you mean?"

"The American," said my companion.

"Hilderman!" I exclaimed. "Surely you must be mistaken. Why, he was absolutely astonished when we told him. He can't have known."

"Still," Garnesk insisted, "I felt sure he knew. I suspected something about him, but I was wrong to do that, quite wrong; I admit that now. I couldn't at first see why he pretended he hadn't heard that Sholto was blind. You may have noticed that I tried to give him the impression that I had examined Miss McLeod and come to the conclusion that I could do nothing. I confess I did that to see how he took it. But I was on a wrong scent altogether. He knew about the dog, that was obvious, but it was also obvious that he hadn't been told from an official source, so to speak. He kept fishing for information.

He brought up the dog several times, each time with a query mark in his voice—as you might say. He remarked that the *last* time he saw Miss McLeod she had her beautiful dog with her. That made me suspicious, because from what you told me she always had her dog with her. Then he said her dog must be feeling it very keenly, you remember. I tried him with my pessimistic conclusions to see how he took it. You see, as soon as I saw the dog I put contagious disease out of the question. Natural forces unguided seemed impossible, but natural forces of some nature that we can't yet understand seemed probable. Still I was wrong to suspect Hilderman, quite wrong. Besides he couldn't possibly have stolen the dog."

"I'm glad you feel you were wrong there," I said, "because I rather like the man. I shouldn't care to have to suspect him."

"Don't suspect him, whatever you do," said the oculist earnestly. "Whatever you do, don't do that. He might be very useful. Make a friend of him. You'll want all your friends."

He rose and stretched his legs, and I followed suit. We stood for a moment on the Chemist's Rock and gazed up the river, over the top of the falls, into the silver and purple symphony of a highland night. Presently my companion turned and took my arm.

"I've seen all I want to see," he said as he began to lead me down to the pool again. "They'll wonder what has become of us. And as I've seen enough for one night, let's get back to the house."

"It's a wonderful view at any time of the day or night," I agreed, and I sighed as I thought of poor Myra.

"It must be," said Garnesk absently, picking his way across the rocks. "It must be a magnificent view. I haven't noticed it; you must bring me here to-morrow."

CHAPTER VIII. MISTS OF UNCERTAINTY

When we got back to the house we found Myra and her father—not unnaturally—wondering what had become of us.

"What have you been doing, and where have you been, and what do you mean by it?" she asked, playfully. "I wish I could see you. I'm sure you must be looking very guilty."

Garnesk and I exchanged hurried glances. It was obvious from her remark that the General had not told her of Sholto's disappearance. I decided there and then that I would have to tell her the whole truth myself, and I gave the others a pretty broad hint that we would like to be left alone. I left the drawing-room and went with them to the library, and answered the old man's feverish questions as to the result of our search.

Then I returned to Myra. It was a difficult and unpleasant task that I had to perform, but I got through it somehow; and, as I expected, Myra was very distressed about her dog, but not in the least frightened. I had thought it wiser not to acquaint her with the specialist's deductions as to the connection between her own affliction and the theft of Sholto. When I had given her as many particulars as I thought advisable, the other two rejoined us.

"Can you think of anyone at all, Miss McLeod," the specialist asked, "who would be likely to steal Sholto?"

"I can't," the girl replied helplessly. "I wish I could."

"The two classes of people we want to find," I suggested, "are those who like Sholto so much as to be prepared to steal him, and those who dislike him so much as to be anxious to destroy him."

"You don't think they'll hurt him," she cried, anxiously. "Poor old fellow! It's bad enough his being blind; but I would rather know he was dead than being ill-treated."

"It's much more likely to be the act of some very human person who covets his neighbour's goods," said Garnesk, reassuringly. "But, at the same time, we must not overlook the other possibility. Can you remember anyone who does dislike the dog?"

"Only one," said Myra, thoughtfully, "and I don't think he could have done it. He has a small croft away up above Tor Beag, and Sholto and I were up there one day; but it's months ago. Sholto went nosing round as usual, and the man came out and got very excited in Gaelic—and you know how excited one can be in that language. He was very rude to me about the dog, and it made me rather suspicious. I told daddy about it after."

"Yes, and I hope you won't go wandering about so far from home without saying where you're going in future, my dear; because——" said the old man, and pulled himself up in pained confusion as he realised the tragic significance of his words.

"Some sort of poacher, perhaps," suggested Garnesk, coming quickly to the rescue.

"An illicit whisky still somewhere about, more likely," Myra replied. And as she could think of no other likely person, and the crofter seemed out of the question, we had to confess ourselves puzzled. I had hoped that Myra would have been able to give us some clue with which we could have satisfied her, while we kept our suspicions to ourselves. Then we left Myra with the specialist, who made a temporary examination. In twenty minutes he assured us that he could make nothing of the case, but that he was willing to stake his reputation that there was nothing organically wrong; and he gave us, so far as he dared, distinct reason to hope that she would eventually regain full possession of her lost faculty. So, after general rejoicings all round, in which I quite forgot the mystery of the man who stole the dog, I went to bed feeling ten years younger, and slept like a top.

When I awoke in the morning much of my elation of spirit had evaporated, and I felt again the oppression of surrounding tragedy. I got up immediately—it was just after six—dressed, and went down to bathe. I was strolling down the drive, with a towel round my neck, when Garnesk put his head out of his window and shouted that he would join me. The tide being in, we saved ourselves a walk to the diving-rock, as the point was called, and bathed from the landing-stage. Refreshed by the swim, we determined to scour the country-side for any tracks of the thief.

"What beats me is how anybody in a place like this, where everybody for miles round knows more about you than you do yourself, could get rid of an enormous beast like Sholto. He was big even for a Dane, and his weight must have been tremendous when he was drugged," said Garnesk, as we walked up the beach path. "Have you ever tried to carry a man who's fainted?"

"I have," I answered with feeling, "and I quite agree with you. If the thief wanted to do away with the dog the beast's body is probably somewhere near."

"What about the river?" my companion suggested.

"More likely the loch," I decided, "or the sea. But that would mean a boat, because it would have to be buried in deep water, or the body would be washed up again on the rocks, even with a heavy weight attached. There are many deep pools in the river, but they are constantly fished, and that would lead to eventual detection. We are dealing with a man who knows his way about. It might be the loch or one of the burns, easily."

Accordingly we decided to try the loch first; but though we followed the path from the house, carefully studying the ground every foot of the way, and examined the banks equally carefully, we were forced to the conclusion that we were on the wrong scent. Then we came down one of the burns that runs from the loch to the sea, and met with the same result.

"We'll walk along the beach and go up the next stream," Garnesk suggested. "Hullo," he exclaimed suddenly, as we clambered over the huge rocks into a tiny cove, "there's been a boat in here!"

I looked at the shingly beach, and saw the keel-marks of a boat and the footprints of its occupants in the middle of the cove. We went up gingerly, for fear of disturbing the ground of our investigations. I looked at the marks, and pondered them for a moment. By this time my senses were wide awake.

"What do you make of it?" the oculist asked.

"Well," I replied, with an apologetic laugh, "I'm afraid you'll think me more picturesque than businesslike if I tell you all the conclusions I've already come to; but the man who came ashore in this boat didn't steal Sholto."

"Go on," he said. "Why, I told you I knew you weren't a fool."

"Thank you!" I laughed. "It seems to me that if a man arrived in a boat and went ashore to steal a dog, he would go away again in the same boat."

"And didn't he?"

"I feel convinced he didn't," I replied, and pointed out to him what must have been obvious to both of us. "Compare the keel-marks with high-water mark. There is less than half a boat's length of keel-mark, and it is just up above high-water mark. This craft, which appears to have been a small rowing-boat, was run ashore at high tide, or very near it, and run out again very quickly. It might conceivably have come in and been caught up by the sea. But Sholto was stolen between a quarter past eight and half-past nine, when the tide was well on the way out. If Sholto went out to sea it was not in this boat."

"Well," said Garnesk, thoughtfully, "your point is good enough for me. We must look somewhere else."

"I hope my attempts at detective work will not put us off the scent," I said, doubtfully.

"I don't think they will, Ewart," said my companion, graciously. "Not in this case, anyway. I'm sure you're right, because this bay can be seen from the top windows of the house."

"You evidently reached my conclusions with half the effort in half the time," I laughed.

"Oh, nonsense!" he exclaimed. "It was you who pointed out that the one man in this boat came in daylight."

"Why 'one man' so emphatically?" I asked.

"When two men come in a boat to commit a theft, and only one of them goes ashore, the other would hardly be expected to sit in the boat and twiddle his thumbs. It's a thousand pounds to a penny that he would get out and walk about the beach. Now, only one gentleman came ashore from this boat, and only one got on board again. One set of footprints going and one coming decided me on that. Besides, if anyone came along and saw a solitary man sitting in a boat, they might ask him how his wife and children were, and he would have to reply; whereas an empty boat, being unable to answer questions, would raise no suspicions."

"You seem to be arguing that this boat may have been the one we are looking for," I pointed out; "and yet we are agreed that the state of the tide made it impossible for Sholto to have been taken away in it."

"Yes," said Garnesk, "I agree to that. But I fancy the thief came by that boat. It seems to me that our man jumps out of the boat, runs ashore, and his friend pulls away and picks him up elsewhere— probably nearer the house. It would look perfectly natural for a man who has apparently been giving a companion a pull across from Skye, say, to land him and then go back. The more I think of this the more it interests me. You see, if the top windows of the house can be seen from the bay, it means that the lower windows can be seen from the top of the cliff. If we can find where our thief lay in wait on the cliff and watched the house, probably with his eyes glued on the dining-room windows to see when we commenced dinner, if we can also find where he left his sea-boots while he went to the house, and then where he rejoined his companion, we are getting on."

"What makes you say 'sea-boots'?" I asked. "You can't tell a top-boot by the footmarks."

"Indirectly you can," Garnesk replied, puffing thoughtfully at his pipe. "That boat was pulled in and pushed out by a man who exerted hardly any pressure, although the beach only slopes gently. His companion did not lend a hand by pushing her out with an oar; if he had done so we should have seen the marks, and I couldn't find any. The only other way to account for it is that our friend, who exerted so little pressure, was wearing sea-boots and walked into the water with the boat. Had he been alone, the jerk of his final jump into the boat would have left a deeper impression on the beach. The tide was just going out; it would have no time to wash this mark away. I looked for the mark, and it wasn't there; so I came to the final conclusion that two men arrived in the cove shortly after seven last night in a small open boat. One of them—a tall, left-handed man in sea-boots—pushed the boat out again and went ashore."

I am afraid I was rude enough to shout with laughter at this very definite statement; but it was mainly with excited admiration that I laughed—certainly not with ridicule. Garnesk turned to me apologetically.

"I know it sounds far-fetched, my dear chap," he said; "but we shall have to think a lot over this business, and I am simply thinking aloud in order

that you can give me your help in my own
conclusions."

"My dear fellow," I cried, "don't, for heaven's
sake, imagine that I am laughing at you. It was the
left-handed touch that made me guffaw with sheer
excitement."

"Well, I think he was left-handed, because the
footmarks were going ashore on the right-hand side
of the keel-marks, and going seawards on the left-
hand side. Jump out of a boat and push it out to sea,
and notice which side of the boat you stand by
instinct—provided you were doing as he was,
pushing on the point of the bows. The fact that his
feet obliterate the keel-marks in one place proves
that. So now we want to find a left-handed man in
sea-boots who knew Sholto was blind"—and he
laughed in a half-apology.

"What about these sea-boots," I asked, "and the
place we are to find where he left them?"

"We'll look for that now; and if we find it we can
be pretty sure our mariner stole the dog."

"You seem to be taking it for granted already," I
pointed out.

"The easiest way to prove he didn't is to satisfy
ourselves that there's no evidence he did," said the
oculist. "But I fancy he did."

"From the way you've sized it up so far I should
be inclined to back your fancy," I admitted frankly. "I
take it, from your diagnosis, that our nautical friend
came ashore here, went up on to the cliff, and glued
his eye to the dining-room window. When he saw we
were at dinner, and it was getting dusk—in fact,
almost dark—he took off his sea-boots and slipped
up to the Lodge in his stocking-soles. So if we climb

the cliff, we expect to find the spot on which he deposited his boots."

"If we expected that," Garnesk replied, "we should also expect to find his boots; and he wouldn't be likely to leave such incriminating evidence in our hands as that. No, my dear Ewart; when he left the cliff he was wearing his boots, and he left them at some point on the path between the house and his embarking place. Come—let's look."

I was intensely interested in my friend's deductions, and I felt convinced that he was right. So we climbed the cliff, he by one route and I by another, in order to see if we could find any traces of last night's visitor. But that was impossible; the rocks were too storm-swept to harbour any sort of lichen which would have shown evidence of footmarks. Still, we were not disappointed when we reached the top, and Garnesk looked at me with a charming expression of boyish triumph when we came across a patch of ground where the heather had obviously been trampled about and worn down by someone recently lying there.

"I don't think we'll worry about tracing him from here just now," said the specialist. "It would be a very difficult job, and we may as well make for the most likely spot to embark from."

"Right you are," I agreed. "I think there can only be one—that is a secluded little inlet, almost hidden by the rocks on the other side of the house."

"Come on, let's have a look at it," my companion urged; and we blundered down the side of the cliff and hurried along the shore. But when we came to the small bay which I had in mind there was certainly some sign of disturbance among the rough gravel with which the shore was carpeted; and that was all the evidence we could find.

"It is such an ideal spot for the job that this almost knocks our theory on the head," murmured Garnesk ruefully. "There are no boat-marks, or anything."

"Which, in a way, bears out your diagnosis," I cried, suddenly hitting on what I thought to be the solution of the difficulty.

"How, in heaven's name?"

"Our old friend the tide," I declared, with returning confidence.

"Of course," he almost shouted. "I've got you, Ewart. The boat came in here while the tide was going out—when, in fact, it was some distance out, possibly nearly an hour after it ran into the other cove. Since then the tide has come in again and obliterated any marks the men may have made. If we find any evidence on a line running between this place and the house, we can call it a certainty."

In feverish excitement we hurried towards the house, casting anxious glances to right and left, but the stubborn heather showed no sign of any recent passenger that way. At last Garnesk, who was some distance to my right, hailed me with an exultant shout. There, sure enough, was a broad patch bearing marks of recent occupation, much the same as the other at the top of the cliff. We were able easily to distinguish the exact spot where the thief had laid the unconscious dog while he put on his boots. The discovery of an unmistakable footprint in a more marshy spot, which could only have been imprinted by a stockinged foot, completed my friend's triumph.

"My dear fellow," I cried heartily, slapping my companion on the back, "I congratulate you. If you go on like this we shall have the dog and the thief in no time."

"It will be some days, even at this rate," he warned me solemnly, "before we get as far as that. Now, back to the embarking-point, and see if we can reconstruct the thing fully."

So we retraced our steps, and studied the shingle once more, but failed to discover any marks of any value. Then we sat down, and the oculist drew a vivid picture of the journey the thief had made. At last, feeling more than satisfied with our work, we rose to go in to breakfast.

"Ewart, I want you to wire for that friend of yours before you do anything else. You may want him soon. I will leave by the morning train to-morrow, but I shall continue on this case till the mystery is solved. In the meantime, you will need someone you can trust at your side all the time."

"I'll go into Glenelg, and wire immediately after breakfast," I promised. "Hullo, more reflections," I laughed, and pointed to a small, bright object some distance away on the rocks, which was catching the glint of the sun.

"We seem to be surrounded by a spying army of glittering objects," laughed my companion, as we strolled on. We had walked some forty yards when some instinct—I know not what—prompted me to investigate the affair. I turned back, and went to pick up the shining object, though for the life of me I could not have told you what I expected to find.

"Garnesk!" I bawled. "Garnesk! Come here!"

"What is it?" he shouted to me, as he came hurtling over the rocks.

"Look at it," I replied tersely, and placed it in his outstretched palm. He glanced at it, and then at me.

"That settles it," he said, and whistled softly, for I had found a small piece of brass, and on it was engraved:—

"Sholto, The Douglas, Invermalluch Lodge, Inverness-shire."

It was the name-plate from Sholto's collar.

Chapter IX. The Mystery Of Sholto

We discussed our discovery pretty thoroughly on the way back to the house, and both agreed that it left no doubt upon one aspect of this strange affair—the man who stole Sholto was no ordinary thief.

The General was standing on the verandah, looking about for us, as we came up the beach path. I told him of Garnesk's deductions and their interesting result, and the old man was greatly affected.

"I never dreamt I should live to see the old place abused in this shocking manner," he grunted. "'Pon me soul, it's—it's begad disgraceful. I've lived here all my life, on and off, and I've never been troubled with anything like this, scarcely so much as a tramp even. I hope to God it'll soon be over, that's all."

"Thanks to Mr. Garnesk, we're moving along in the right direction," I tried to reassure him. "And we have the satisfaction, in one way, of being able to tell Myra that Sholto is still alive, even if we don't know where he is."

"Seems to me, Ronald," said the General, "you don't know that, or anything about the poor beast, except that he has been stolen, and probably taken away in a boat. Judging by Mr. Garnesk's theory, they probably threw him overboard in deep water."

"No one who intended destroying a dog would take the trouble to wrench the name-plate off his collar," I pointed out. "The dog is alive, and not unconscious. They need his collar to keep him in hand, but they are afraid the plate might give them away. Mr. Garnesk is right, I'm sure, and if we find the thief we find the cause for Myra's terrible misfortune."

"Where do you imagine they can have taken him to then? Seems to me we're getting some pretty queer neighbours."

"That is just what we have to find out," said Garnesk, "and I for one will not rest until I do."

"'Pon my soul, my dear chap," said the old man warmly, "it's very good of you to take so much interest in the affairs of total strangers. It is, indeed, thundering good of you."

"Not at all, General," laughed the visitor. "If you spent your life trying to cure fussy ladies of imaginary eye trouble, without putting it to them that their livers are out of order, you'd welcome this as a very appetising antidote."

"Talking about appetites," his host suggested, "who says breakfast?"

"I fancy we both do," I answered, and we turned indoors.

During breakfast Garnesk announced his determination to devote as much of the day as necessary to an examination of Myra, and then catch the evening train from Mallaig, but the girl herself rose in rebellion at this immediately.

"You mustn't do anything of the sort," she declared emphatically. "Daddy, tell him he's not to. The idea of coming up here, and looking at me, and then going away again! It's ridiculous!"

"I assure you, it is ample reward," declared the oculist gallantly, and everybody laughed at the frank compliment.

"But you must fish the river, have a day on the loch. Ron must take you in the motor-boat up to Kinlochbourn. Then you've simply got to see Scavaig and Coruisk—oh! and a hundred other things besides."

Garnesk insisted that, much as he would like to stay, he felt bound to leave at once, but Myra was equally obstinate; and, as was natural, being a woman, she won on a compromise. Garnesk agreed to stay over the week-end. I was very glad that Myra liked my new friend. She had been very shy of Olvery, but she took an immediate fancy to the Glasgow specialist. She liked his voice, she told me afterwards, and on the second day of his visit she asked him if his sister was very much younger than he. Garnesk looked up in surprise.

"One of them is," he replied, "nearly twenty years. What made you ask?"

"I guessed it by the way you talk to me," Myra declared confidently.

"The detective instinct seems to be in the air," I laughed.

So when I borrowed Angus's ramshackle old cycle, and went into Glenelg along a road which is more noteworthy for its picturesqueness than its navigable qualities, I left Garnesk to his examination with the knowledge that he would do his utmost, and that she would help him all she could.

I wired to Dennis: "I can meet you at Mallaig Monday morning. Wire reply.—RONALD." Then I sent a couple of picture postcards to Tommy and Jack, wishing them luck, and explaining that I had not returned to join them because Myra was ill. I was sure Dennis would appreciate the urgency of my message, but I worded it carefully, deliberately making it appear to be the answer to an inquiry, for the reason that it is always wise to do as little as you can to stimulate local gossip. Anything like "Come at once; most urgent," despatched by one who was known to be a visitor at the lodge, would have set the entire country-side talking. So I jumped on to Angus's collection of old metal, and jolted back again as fast as I could. Garnesk was still engaged with Myra, and I took the opportunity of a chat with her father.

"Would you care to see the discoveries we made this morning?" I asked, when I found him in the library.

"Yes, I should indeed, my boy," he responded eagerly, and I think he was glad of the diversion. "I'll come with you now."

"There is one thing I want to say, sir, before we go any farther."

"What is it?" he asked, looking rather anxiously at me.

"I want to tell you," I said, "that in the event of Myra not regaining her sight I should like your permission to marry her as soon as she herself wishes it. As you know, I have a small private income, which is sufficient for my needs in London, and would be more than I should require up here. If Myra is to be blind, I should like to marry her in order that I may always be able to take care of her, and I should propose to settle down somewhere near you. I dabble in contributory journalism, and I could extend that as far as possible, and I might even do pretty well at it. Both she and you would know then that, in the event of anything happening to you, she would be cared for by someone she loves."

"My dear Ronald," exclaimed the old man, affectionately laying a hand on my shoulder, "I'm very glad to hear you say that. As a matter of fact, whatever happens, I don't care how soon you marry my dear girl. She wants it with all her heart, and I have always been fond of you myself. The only thing that has held me back up to now is the question of money, and, possibly, a little selfishness. I'm not a rich man, as you know, and if it were not for my pension I couldn't even live in my father's house. But now my one desire is to see my poor little girl happy, and we'll scrape together a shilling or two somehow. Shake hands, my boy."

We both of us forgot all about the terrible war, and, naturally enough, the mysterious trouble which faced us then was sufficient for the moment. Having settled that question at last, I conducted the old man to the small cove where we had made our first discovery, but we began by visiting the coach-house. I daresay that to the trained eye there may have been valuable evidence lying under our very noses, but the only confused marks which we found on the surrounding ground conveyed nothing to either of us. Later, on our way back to the house, from what we now called "the embarking-point," we came upon a spot where the heather had been cut off in fairly large quantities. The old man stood, and contemplated the shorn stumps for a moment, and shook his head solemnly. It was not that he had any sentimental regret for the heather which grew on almost every inch of ground for hundreds of miles round, but he objected to the sign of visitors, or, as he would have said, "trippers."

"Who would want to cut heather here?" I asked, for I could not see the slightest reason for gathering anything which could be obtained at your door wherever you lived in the Highlands.

"Holiday-makers," he said ruefully. "They take rooms in the village, and get it into their heads that the heather in one spot is better than anything else for miles round, so they walk out to that spot, and cut some to take away with them when they go back home. I wish they'd always go back home and stop there."

When I showed the General the keel-marks in the cove and explained to him in detail how Garnesk had arrived at his conclusions, the old man was quite awed.

"'Pon me soul, he must be thundering clever, thundering clever," he muttered. "But it's not healthy, you know, Ronald; in fact, it's begad unhealthy. I've always been a bit scared of these people who see things that are not there. Still, I suppose it's the modern way; reading all these detective yarns and so on does it, no doubt."

He was still marvelling at this new mystery when we got back to the house to find Myra sitting on the verandah with the specialist, who was keeping her in fits of laughter with anecdotes of some of his wealthy women patients.

He sprang up as he saw us approaching, and ran down to meet us.

"I'm certain of one thing," he said excitedly, as he walked between us, and answered the General's question. "We have got to solve the mystery, and she will see again. This is something new, but it has a very simple solution, which we must find out by hook or by crook. When I know how Miss McLeod lost her sight I shall very likely be able to find out how to restore it, and I shall also know something that perhaps no other oculist has ever dreamed of. There isn't the slightest sign of any organic disease, which probably means that Nature will assert herself, and she will eventually regain her sight naturally. But we mustn't wait for that. We've got to be up and doing. I tell you, sir, I wouldn't have missed this for anything. Have you been exploring?"

"We've been having a look at those marks which meant so much to you and conveyed nothing whatever to me, although I was once considered something of a scout," the General admitted.

"Did you find anything fresh?"

"No, only some trippers, as the General calls them, had been cutting heather," I replied.

"That's not likely to help us much," the oculist agreed, "unless they were not trippers at all, and were cutting the heather as a blind. What were they like?"

"Oh, we didn't see them. We only saw the results of their iconoclasm. The heather was recently, but not freshly, cut," I replied, and the old man glanced at me with some slight suspicion, as if he feared I, too, was about to take up the deduction business.

"Recent, but not fresh?" muttered Garnesk.

"Now, why should a man who wanted——Good heavens! I've got it."

"What *are* you dear people getting so excited about?" Myra asked, for by this time we had almost reached the verandah.

"We'll tell you in a minute, dear," I called, and waited for Garnesk to explain.

"Of course," he continued, as if thinking aloud, "it's obvious. The man came ashore in a small boat, picked some heather, and carried it in his arms. Anyone who noticed him would have noticed his load of heather. Then he stole Sholto, concealed him under the heather, and was still apparently only carrying a bundle of innocent heath. Why! they seem to have thought of everything, and made no mistake."

"Except that the man was wandering about the country-side, gathering wild flowers, in his stockinged soles," I pointed out.

"Still, it was almost dark, and he chanced that," said Garnesk.

"What I don't understand about it is this," the General joined in: "Where did he come from to gather this heather? A man must know that if he is seen to come ashore and pick heather and get into his boat again he is doing a very curious thing. That boat can only have come from Knoydart or Skye at the farthest, and everybody knows you wouldn't take heather there."

"Yes, I'm afraid you're right, General," Garnesk admitted, with a sigh of regret, and I was compelled to agree with him.

"I know where he came from, then."

It was said so quietly that it startled us all, though it was Myra who spoke.

"Where, then?" we all asked together.

"He must have come from a yacht."

Chapter X: The Secret Of The Rock

We made exhaustive inquiries everywhere, but no one had seen a yacht anchored or otherwise resting off the point the previous night. One or two vessels had been noticed passing the mouth of Loch Hourn during the evening, but they were mostly recognisable as belonging to residents in the neighbourhood, and in any case not one of them had been seen to drop the two men in a boat who were causing us so much anxiety. When Garnesk and I went up the river to the Chemist's Rock we were equally unsuccessful there.

"Look here," I said, "suppose you were to go blind, Mr. Garnesk? I can't allow you to run any risks of that sort. We have every reason to know that there is something gruesome and uncanny about this spot, and I should feel happier if you would keep at a safe distance."

"How about yourself?" he replied.

"It's a personal affair with me," I pointed out, "but I can't let your kindness in assisting us as you are doing run the length of possible blindness."

"Nonsense, my dear fellow," he exclaimed; "we're in this together. I am just as keen to get to the bottom of this matter as you are. But it behoves us both to be careful. It is most important that you should take care of yourself at the present moment. What would happen to Miss McLeod if I carried you back to the house in a state of total blindness?"

"Oh, I shall be all right," I declared confidently. "But, of course, your point is a good one, and I shall not run any risks."

"And yet you start by careering up the river here when we have very excellent reasons for supposing that it is hardly the place to spend a quiet afternoon."

"You don't really believe that there is anything curious about the river itself, do you?" I asked. "We have agreed that some human agency is responsible for the tragic affliction that has fallen upon poor Myra. In that case we are not safe anywhere."

"That's true enough," he agreed, "but everything that has happened so far has happened here. Sooner or later, no doubt, the operations will be extended to some other region, but at present we know there is a possibility of our being overcome by some strange peril between the Chemist's Rock and Dead Man's Pool."

"Well, as we don't know how to deal with the danger when it does arrive," I suggested, "suppose we see as much as we can from the banks. I will go up the centre of the stream and report to you, if you like, but you stay here."

"You'll do nothing of the sort," he cried. "I can't imagine what we can possibly learn by standing on that rock, but if either of us goes, we go together, or I, in my capacity of bachelor unattached, go alone."

Naturally, I could only applaud such generous sentiments, and at the same time refuse to countenance his proposal. So we sat among the heather, some distance above the bank, and awaited developments.

"It is four-twenty now," said my companion presently, looking at his watch. "If anything is going to happen it should happen soon."

"Don't you think it was mere coincidence that Myra's blindness and the General's strange illusion occurred about this time? Why should this green ray only be visible between four and five?"

"It hasn't really been visible at all," Garnesk pointed out. "Miss McLeod saw a green flash, and the General saw a green rock, which had taken upon itself the responsibilities of transportation. That's all we know about the green ray, except the green veil that Miss McLeod tells us of. I don't expect to see that."

"I wish I knew what we did expect to see," I sighed.

"Exactly," he replied solemnly. "By the way," he added after a pause, "do you see anything peculiar about the rocks or the pool between four and five; I mean anything that you couldn't notice at any other time of the day?"

"Nothing at all," I answered despondently; "it is pleasanter here then than at any other time—or was until we came under this mysterious spell."

"Why is it pleasanter?" he asked.

"It is just then that it gets most sunshine," I pointed out.

I made the remark idly enough, for the course of the river, with its rugged banks and great massive rocks, looked particularly beautiful as the sun streamed full upon it, and I was immeasurably surprised when Garnesk jumped to his feet with a shout.

"What is it?" I cried in alarm. "You're not——"

"The sun, Ewart, the sun!" he exclaimed, and, snatching a pair of binoculars which I carried in my hand, he dashed up the slope to the foot of a cliff that overhung the stream. I gazed after him for a moment in astonishment, and then set out in pursuit.

"Stop where you are, man!" he called to me as he turned, and saw me tearing after him. "No, no; I want you there. Don't follow me."

I did as I was told, for I trusted him implicitly, and I knew that he would not run any risk without first acquainting me of his intention, and I took it for granted that he had arranged a part for me to play, although he had not had time to tell me what it was. But my astonishment increased as I watched him climb the rock, for when he arrived a few feet from the summit he sat down on a ledge and calmly lighted a cigarette!

"What is it all about?" I called to him, when I had fully recovered from my surprise.

"I only wanted to have a look at the view," he laughed back, and put the glasses to his eyes. First he examined the house, and then he turned his gaze in the direction of the sea. It was then that it dawned on me that he was looking for a yacht. This was the fateful hour, and it had naturally struck him that the unknown yacht might be in the vicinity.

"Well," I shouted, "can you see the yacht?"

"No," he replied, "there's nothing in sight, only a paddle steamer; looks like an excursion of some sort."

"Oh! that's the *Glencoe*," I explained; "she won't help us at all. She runs with tourists from Mallaig."

"She seems to be barely able to take care of herself," he laughed. "I shouldn't like to be on her in a storm."

We conversed fairly easily while he was on the cliff, for we were not many yards apart, and I began to wonder when he was coming down again.

"Have you any objection to my joining you?" I asked presently, as there seemed to be nothing for me to do below.

"Stop where you are for a bit, old man," he advised. "I shall be down in a minute."

"As long as you like," I replied. "You've got a fine view from there, anyway. Don't worry about me."

I sat down on a rock, refilled my pipe, and prepared to wait till he rejoined me.

"Hi! Ewart!" he called presently, for my mind had already wandered to that darkened "den" at the house.

"Hullo," I answered, jumping to my feet. "What is it?"

"Do you notice anything unusual?"

"No," I shouted, "nothing that——," but suddenly I felt a strange singing in my ears, my pulses quickened, my voice died away into nothing. I looked up at Garnesk; he was leaning perilously near the edge of the cliff waving to me. I saw his lips move, yet I heard no sound. My heart was thumping against my chest with audible beats. I looked round me in every direction. No, there was nothing strange happening that the eye could see, yet here was I with a choking pulsation in my throat. My temples too were throbbing like a couple of steam hammers. Again I looked up at Garnesk; he was climbing hurriedly down the cliff. He paused and waved to me, and again his lips moved, and again I heard nothing.

Surely, I told myself, the events of the past few days had told on my strength. This was nerves, sheer nerves. Garnesk must give me his arm to the house. I would lie down and rest, and I should be all right in a few moments. It was nerves, that was all. But if Garnesk were not very quick about it I should have burst a blood-vessel in my brain before he reached me. Already my chest seemed to have swelled to twice its size. Garnesk, as I looked, seemed to be farther off than ever, a tiny speck in the distance.

The singing in my ears became a rushing torrent. It was the waterfall, I told myself; how stupid of me! Of course I should be all right in a minute. But my friend must hurry. I collapsed on the rock and gasped for breath. I looked for Garnesk. Still he seemed to be as far away as ever, and he scarcely seemed to be moving at all. I must tell him to be quick. It was simply nerves, of course; but I mustn't let them get the better of me, or what would poor Myra do? I staggered to my feet to call to Garnesk.

"Hurry up; I'm not well." I framed the words in my brain, but no sound passed my lips. I struggled for breath, and called again with all the power I could muster. I could not hear myself speak. And then I understood! My knees rocked beneath me, the river swirled round me, a rowan tree rushed by me in a flash, and as I fell sprawling on my face among the heather a thousand hammers seemed to pound the hideous sickening truth into the heaving pulp that was once my brain.

Chapter XI. How The Unexpected Happened

When I came to myself I was lying with my head pillowed on Garnesk's arm. My coat and collar were on the ground beside me, and my head and shoulders were dripping with water.

"Ah!" said my companion, with a sigh of relief, "that's better. You'll be all right in a few minutes, Ewart. Take it easy, old chap, and rest."

"Where am I?" I asked. "Good heavens!" I exclaimed, as I heard my own voice, and sat bolt upright in my astonishment, "I thought I was dumb!"

"Well, never mind about that now, old fellow," Garnesk advised. "We'll hear all about that later. Shut your eyes and rest a minute."

"All right," I agreed, "pass me my pipe and I will."

Garnesk laughed aloud as he leaned over to reach my coat pocket.

"When a man shouts for his pipe he's a long way from being dead or dumb or anything else," he said.

Truth to tell, I was feeling very queer. I was dizzy and confused, but I felt that I wanted my pipe to help me collect my thoughts. So I lay there for some minutes quietly smoking, and indeed I felt as if I could have stayed like that for ever.

"I must have fainted," I explained presently, overlooking the fact that Garnesk probably knew more about my ridiculous seizure than I did myself. "I don't know when I did a thing like that before," I added, beginning to get angry with myself.

"Well, I hope you won't do it again," said my
friend fervently. "It's not a thing to make a hobby of.
And don't you come near this infernal river any more
until we know something definite."

"You mean that the place has got on my nerves," I
said. "I suppose it has; I'm very sorry."

"Do you feel well enough to tell me all about it?"
he asked, "or would you rather wait till we get up to
the house?"

"Oh, I'll tell you now," I agreed readily. "We
mustn't say anything about this at the house." So I
told him exactly how I had felt.

"When did it first come on?" he asked.

"When I heard you shout, and jumped up to see
what it was. By the way, what was it?"

"Well," he replied, "we'll discuss the matter if you
wouldn't mind releasing my arm?"

"My dear fellow," I cried, sitting up suddenly, as I
realised that he was still propping up my head, "I'm
most awfully sorry."

"Now then," he said, as he lighted his pipe and
made himself comfortable, "we'll go into the latest
development. You remember what made me rush off
and leave you there?"

"I remember saying something about the
sunlight, and you suddenly dashed off."

"To tell you the truth, I had very little faith in the
theory that at this hour, above all, the spook of the
Chemist's Rock was active, until you pointed out
that only about that time is the whole of the river
course up to the rock, and the whole of the rock
itself, flooded with sunlight. Then, when you made
that remark, I suddenly felt that I ought to be on the
cliff on the look out for this unknown yacht. We

connect the two together in some way which we don't yet understand, so I meant to go and have a look for the ship. I saw nothing of any importance until I shouted to you. Just then I was looking through the glasses at the shore. I turned them on the landing-stage and along the beach, and I had just lighted on the bay where we explored this morning when suddenly, for half a second or so, all the shadows of the rocks turned a vivid green, and then as suddenly resumed their natural colour again."

"Good heavens!" I exclaimed. "Green again! Can you make anything of it at all, Garnesk? I'm sorry I'm such a duffer as to faint at the critical moment, when I might have been of some assistance to you. What in God's name can it all mean?"

"I'm no further on," he replied bitterly; "in fact, I'm further back."

"Further back!" I cried. "How? I don't see how you can be."

"I'll tell you what my theory was about all this affair, and it struck me as a good one—strange, of course, but then, this is a strange business."

"It is, indeed," I agreed ruefully. "Well, go on."

"I had an idea, Ewart, that we should find some sort of wireless telegraphy at the bottom of this business. I had almost made up my mind that we had stumbled across the path of some inventor who was working with a new form of wireless transmission. I felt that in that way we might account for Miss McLeod's blindness and the blindness of the dog. It also seemed to hold good as to the disappearance of Sholto. The inventor hears of the extraordinary effect of his invention, and is afraid he will get into a mess if it is found out. The yacht to experiment from fitted in beautifully. But now all that's knocked on the head."

"Why?" I asked. "It seems to me, Garnesk, that you are doing all the thinking in this affair, as if you had been used to it all your life. Your only trouble is that you're too modest. I take it that because you didn't see the yacht when you noticed the green flash you are taking it for granted you were wrong to expect it. I must say, old chap, I think you've done thundering well, as the General would put it, and even if you are prepared to admit your theory has been knocked on the head I'm not—at any rate, not until I have a jolly good reason. Yet it doesn't seem to matter much what I say or do if I'm going to faint like a girl at the first sign of danger. If you hadn't come to my rescue I might still be lying there waiting to come round, or something," I finished in disgust.

My companion looked at me thoughtfully.

"Ewart," he said, and solemnly shook his head, "you have brought me to the very thing that made me say my theory was exploded."

"What thing?" I asked. "Surely my fainting can't have made any difference to conclusions you had already come to?"

"But then you see," my friend replied, "you didn't faint. And if I had not seen you were in difficulties you would probably never have recovered."

"Didn't faint?" I exclaimed. "Well, I don't know what the medical term for it is, and I daresay there are several technical phrases for the girlish business I went through. That idea of being dumb was simply imagination, but I assure you it was just what I should call a fainting fit."

"I don't want to alarm you if you're not feeling well," he began apologetically.

"Go on," I urged. "I'm as fit as I ever was."

"Well," the young specialist responded, in a serious tone, "if you want to know the truth, Ewart, you were suffocated."

"Suffocated!" I shouted, jumping to my feet. "What in heaven's name do you mean?"

"I can't tell you exactly what I mean because I don't know, but yours was certainly not an ordinary fainting fit. To put the whole thing in non-medical terms, you were practically drowned on dry land!"

I sat down again—heavily at that. Should we never come to an end of these mysterious attacks which were hurled at us in broad daylight from nowhere at all?

"I'm not sure that you hadn't better rest before we go into this fully, Ewart," Garnesk remarked doubtfully. "You're not by any means as fit as you've ever been, in spite of your emphatic assurance."

"Tell me what you think, why you think it, and what you feel we ought to do. Why, man, Myra might have been here alone, with no one to rescue her and—and——"

"Quite so," said Ewart sympathetically. "So you must comfort yourself with the knowledge that it may be a great blessing that she has temporarily lost her sight. Now, I say you didn't faint, because, medically, I know you didn't. For the same reason I say you were suffocating as surely as if you had been drowning. Hang it, my dear chap, it's my line of business, you know. I can't account for it, but there is the naked fact for you."

"How does this affect your previous conclusions?" I asked. "Before you tell me what you think brought on this suffocation I should like to hear why you give up your theory."

"Simply because no wireless, or other electric current, could have that effect upon you. If you had had an electric shock in any of its many curious forms I could have said it bore me out; but, you see, it's impossible. And, as I refuse to believe that we are continually bumping into new mysteries which have no connection with each other, it follows that if this suffocation was not caused by the supposed wireless experiments, the other can't have been either."

"I'm not making the slightest imputation on your medical knowledge," I ventured, "but are you absolutely certain that you are not mistaken?"

"My dear fellow," he laughed, "for goodness sake don't be so apologetic. I can quite see that you find it difficult to believe. But I am prepared to swear to it all the same. For one thing, the symptoms were unmistakable; for another, it seems impossible that we should both faint at exactly the same time and place for no reason at all."

"You didn't faint too, surely?" I cried.

"No," he admitted, "but we might very easily have been suffocated together—smothered as surely as the princes in the Tower. When I saw you were in difficulties I shouted to you. Obviously you didn't hear me. I naturally didn't wait to see what would happen to you; I cleared down the cliff, and sprinted to you as fast as I could. When I came to within about twenty yards of you I found a difficulty in breathing. I went on for a couple of paces, and realised that the air was almost as heavy as water. So I rushed back, undid my collar, took a deep breath; and bolted in to you, picked you up, and carted you here. *Voila!* But I very nearly joined you on the ground, and then we would never have regained consciousness, either of us. I applied the simplest form of artificial respiration to you, dowsed your head, and now you're all right. On the whole, Ewart, we can consider ourselves very well out of this latest adventure."

"What you're really telling me," I pointed out gratefully, "is that you saved my life at the risk of your own. I'm no good at making speeches, or anything of that sort, Garnesk, but I thank you, if you know what that means. And Myra will——"

"Not a word to her, Ewart," my companion interrupted eagerly. "Whatever you do, don't on any account worry that poor girl with this new complication. Anything on earth but that."

"No," I agreed; "you're right there. Myra must be kept in the dark."

"Yes," he replied, with a look of relief. "It might have a serious effect on her chances of recovery if she had this additional worry. And I don't think it would be advisable to tell the old man either. I think we had better keep it to ourselves absolutely. Tell no one, Ewart, except your friend when he comes."

"Very well," I answered, for I was very anxious to spare both Myra and her father from the knowledge of any further trouble. "I'll tell Dennis when he comes, but otherwise it is our secret."

"Good," said Garnesk. "Now put your coat on, old chap, and we'll stroll back to the house."

I got up and buttoned my collar, retied my bow, and slipped into my jacket. I was rather uncomfortably damp, and I felt a bit shaky and queer, and decided that I could do with a complete rest from the mysteries of the green ray. But the subject remained uppermost in my mind, and my tired brain still strove to unravel the tangled threads of the puzzle.

"By the way," I said, as we walked slowly up to the house, "you have not yet explained what there was in my remark about the sunlight that made you think of the yacht."

"Well," he replied, "you see I had an idea that perhaps they might come here when the gorge, through which the river flows, was flooded with light, so that they could see if any strange effects were produced. But that suffocation was not brought about by any electrical experiment, and I am beginning to be afraid that, after all, we may be up against some strange natural phenomena, some terrible combination of the forces of Nature, which has not yet been observed, or at any rate recorded."

"Why afraid?" I asked, for although I had been glad to believe that we were faced with a problem which would prove to have a human solution, the revulsion had come, and I should have welcomed the knowledge that some weird, freakish application of natural power might be held accountable.

"Afraid?" queried Garnesk, with a note of surprise. "I am very often afraid of Nature. She is a devoted slave, but a cruel mistress. I don't think that I should ever be very much scared by a human being, even in his most fiendish aspect, but Nature—I tell you, Ewart, there are things in Nature that make me shudder!"

"Yes," I agreed heavily, "you're right, of course. That's how I have felt for the past twenty-four hours. It was a tremendous relief to me to feel that we were men looking for men. But the last few minutes I have had an idea that it would be comforting to explain it all out of a text-book of physics. Still, you're right. It is better far to be men fighting men than to be puny molecules tossed in the maelstrom of immutable power which created the world, and may one day destroy it."

"I'm glad you agree," he said simply. "You see you could not possibly live for a second in electrically produced atmosphere which was so thick that you couldn't hear yourself speak. Death would be instantaneous. It couldn't have been our unknown professor's wireless experiments after all. Yet it seems impossible that a sudden new power should crop up suddenly at one spot like this. Imagine what would happen if this had occurred in a city, in a crowded street. Hundreds would have been stricken blind, then hundreds would have been suffocated. Vehicles would have run amok, and the result would have been an indescribable chaos of the maimed, mangled and distraught. A flash like this green ray (which blinded Miss McLeod and her dog, deluded the General, and nearly suffocated us) at the mouth of a harbour, say, the entrance to a great port— Liverpool, London, or Glasgow—would be responsible for untold loss of life. If this terrible phenomenon spread, Ewart, it would paralyse the industry of the world in twenty-four hours. If it spread still farther the face of the globe would become the playing-fields of Bedlam in a moment. Think of the result of this everywhere! Some suffocated, some blinded, and millions probably mad and sightless, stumbling over the bodies of the dead to cut each other's throats in the frenzy of sudden imbecility."

"Don't, Garnesk," I begged. "It won't bear thinking about. We have enough troubles here to deal with without that!"

"Yes," my companion admitted, "we need not add to them by any idle conjectures of still more hideous horrors to come. But it is an interesting, if terrible speculation. And it means one thing to us, Ewart, of the very greatest importance. We must solve the riddle somehow."

"You mean," I cried, as I realised the tremendous import of his words—"you mean that the sanity of the universe may rest with us! You mean that if we can solve this riddle we, or others, may be able to devise some means of prevention, or at least protection? You mean that we are in duty bound to keep at this night and day until we find out what it is?"

"That is just what I do mean," he replied seriously. "It is a solemn duty; who knows, it may be a holy trust. Ewart, we agree to get to the bottom of this? We have agreed once, but are we still prepared to go on with this now that we know we may be crushed in the machinery that controls the solar system and lights the very sun?"

"I shall certainly go on," I replied eagerly. "But we can hardly expect you to run risks on our behalf."

"It may be in the interests of civilisation," he answered, "and in that case it is our duty. Now look here, Ewart, this will have to be a secret. It is essential that we should not get ourselves laughed at because, for one thing, the scoffers may get into serious trouble if they start investigating our assertions in a spirit of levity. You and I must keep this to ourselves entirely. What about your friend?"

"I can trust him," I replied simply.

"Then tell him everything," Garnesk advised. "If you know you can rely upon him he may be of great assistance to us."

"What about Hilderman?" I asked. "He knows a good deal already."

"There is no need for him to know any more. He may be of some use to us. I had thought he might be of the greatest use, but he may be able to help us still. We should decrease, rather than augment, his usefulness by telling him these new complications."

"How do you mean?" I asked.

"Well, for instance, he might think we are mad, although he's a very shrewd fellow."

"Yes," I agreed, "I think he's pretty cute. Funny that Americans so often are. Anyway, he's been cute enough to make sufficient to retire on at a fairly early age, and retire comfortably too."

"H'm," was my companion's only comment.

After dinner that evening we discussed all sorts of subjects, mainly the war, of course, and went to bed early.

"Now, Ron," exclaimed Myra, as we said good-night, "if Mr. Garnesk is really going to leave us on Monday, you mustn't let him worry about things to-morrow. Do let him have one day's holiday while he is with us, anyway."

"I will," I agreed. "We'll have a real holiday tomorrow. Suppose we all go up Loch Hourn in the motor-boat in the afternoon?"

So it was arranged that we should have an afternoon on the sea and a morning's fishing on the loch. Garnesk fell in with the idea readily.

"It will do you good," he declared. "You won't be feeling too frisky in the morning after your adventure this afternoon."

As it turned out he was quite right, for I awoke in the morning with a slight headache and a tendency to ache all over. So we fished the loch in a very leisurely fashion for an hour or two, and after lunch the four of us went up to Kinlochbourn. We took a tea-basket with us, and very nearly succeeded in banishing the green ray altogether from our minds. I had taken my Kodak with me, and we ran in shore, and otherwise altered our course occasionally in order to enable me to record some choice peep of the magnificent scenery. When we got back to the lodge we were all feeling much the better for the outing. After dinner Myra, who had taken the greatest interest in the photographs, although, poor child, she could not see what I had taken, and would not be able to see the result either, was anxious to know how they had turned out.

"I should love to know if the snapshots are good," she said, "particularly the one at Caolas Mor. Develop them in the morning, Ronnie, won't you? If you don't you'll probably take them away, and forget all about them."

Garnesk looked at me. He was always on the *qui vive* for any opportunity to give Myra a little pleasure. He felt very strongly that she must be kept from worrying at all costs.

"Why not develop them now, Ewart?" he suggested.

"Certainly," I said, "if everybody will excuse me."

"Dad's in the library," Myra replied, "but everybody else will come with you if you ask us nicely. Besides, I shall have to tell you where everything is. There's plenty of room for us all."

"Right you are," I agreed readily, and went out to get a small folding armchair from the verandah. We went up to the dark-room at the top of the house, and Myra sat in the corner, giving me instructions as to the position of the bottles, etc. I prepared the developer while Garnesk busied himself with the fixing acid.

"Now we're ready," I announced, as I made sure that the light-tight door was closed, and lowered the ruby glass over the orange on Myra's imposing dark-room lamp; she believed in doing things comfortably; no messing about with an old-fashioned "hock-bottle" for her. I took the spool from my pocket and began to develop them *en bloc*.

"How are they coming along?" Myra asked, leaning forward interestedly.

"They're beginning to show up," I replied; "they look rather promising."

"It's rather warm in here," said the girl presently; "do you think it would matter if I removed my shade, Mr. Garnesk?"

"Not if you put it on again before we put the light up," the specialist answered. Myra took off the shade and the heavy bandage with a sigh of relief, and leaned her elbow on the table beside her.

"There's a glass beaker just by your arm, dear," I said; "just a minute and I'll put it out of reach."

"All right," said Garnesk, moving forward, "I'll move it; don't you worry."

But before he could reach the table there was a crash. The beaker went smashing to the floor. I turned with a laugh, which died on my lips. Myra was standing up with her hand to her head.

"What is it, darling?" I cried, dropping the length of film on the floor. Garnesk made a grab for the shade. Myra gave a short, shrill little laugh, which had a slightly ominous, hysterical note in it.

"Don't be alarmed, dear," she said quietly, in a curiously tense voice, "*I can see!*"

CHAPTER XII. WHO IS HILDERMAN?

I must admit that I was so delighted to find that Myra had recovered her sight that I very nearly made what might have been a very serious mistake. I gave a loud shout of triumph and made a dive for the light, intending to switch it on. This might, of course, have had a very bad effect upon my darling's eyes, but fortunately Garnesk darted across the room and knocked up my arm in the nick of time.

"Not yet, Ewart, not yet," he warned me. "We must run no risks until we are quite sure."

"But, Ronnie, I can see quite well," Myra declared delightedly. "I see everything just as easily as I usually can by the light of the dark-room lamp."

"Still, we won't expose you to the glare of white light just at present, Miss McLeod," said Garnesk solemnly. "We must be very careful. Tell me, how did your sight return, gradually or suddenly?"

"Suddenly, I think," the girl replied. "I took off the shade and laid it down, and then when I looked up I could distinctly see the lamp."

"Immediately the shade was removed?"

"No," she answered, "not just immediately. You see, I was looking at the floor, which is so dark, of course, that you couldn't see it in the ordinary way. Then as soon as I looked up I could see the lamp. For a moment I thought it was my imagination, but when I found I could see Ron stooping over the developing-dish I knew that I was all right again."

"This is very extraordinary, you know," said Garnesk. "Can you count the bottles on the middle shelf?"

"Oh, yes!" laughed Myra, "I can make them out distinctly. Of course, I know pretty well what they are, but in any case I could easily describe them to you if I'd never seen them before."

"What have I got in my hand?" the specialist queried, holding his arm out.

"A pair of nail-clippers," Myra declared emphatically, and Garnesk laughed.

"Well," he said, "you can obviously see it pretty well; but, as a matter of fact, it's a cigar-cutter."

"Oh! well, you see," the girl explained airily, "I always put necessity before luxury!"

So then the oculist made her sit down again and questioned and cross-questioned her at considerable length.

"I'm puzzled, but delighted," he admitted finally. "It's strange, but it is at the same time decidedly hopeful."

"I suppose it means that she will always be able to see in a red light at any rate?" I suggested.

"Probably it does," he agreed, "and, of course, her sight may be completely restored. There is also a middle course; she may be able to see perfectly after a course of treatment in red light. I will get her a pair of red glasses made at once. We can see how that goes. But I feel that it would be advisable to introduce her to daylight in gradual stages, in case of any risk."

"Oh, if we could only find poor old Sholto!" Myra exclaimed eagerly. Garnesk turned to her with a look of frank admiration.

"You're a lucky young dog, Ewart," he whispered to me, "by Jove you are!"

So Myra graciously, but a little regretfully I think, placed herself in the hands of the young specialist and replaced her shade. Then we left the dark-room, allowing the films to develop out on the floor, and went downstairs. We took her out on to the verandah and removed the shade for a moment, but the chill air of the highland night made her eyes smart after their unaccustomed imprisonment, and we gave up the experiment for that night.

As Garnesk and I bathed together in the morning we were both brighter and more cheerful than we had been since his arrival.

"I shall catch the train from Mallaig," he declared. "Can you take me in and meet your friend without having long to wait?"

"If you insist on going," I replied, "I can get you there in time to meet him and you will have an hour or more to wait for your train."

"Oh, so much the better! We can tell him everything and give him all the news in the interval."

"Are you still determined to go?" I asked.

"Yes," he said, "I *must* go. It will be necessary for me to make one or two inquiries and get a pair of glasses made for Miss McLeod."

"I shall be very sorry to lose you, Garnesk," I said earnestly. "Don't you think you could write or wire for the glasses? You see, if we have come to the conclusion that this green ray is some chemical production of Nature unassisted there isn't the same reason for you to leave us."

"No, that's true," he agreed, "but we were both a bit scared yesterday, old chap, and the more I think of this dog business the less I like it. It was mere conceit on my part that made me say it was bound to be some natural phenomenon merely because I couldn't understand how the effect could have been humanly produced."

"Perhaps," I suggested, "our best course would be to keep an open mind about the whole thing."

"Yes," he replied, "I'm with you entirely. And in that case my going away is not going to aggravate the effects of a natural phenomenon, while it may restrain the human agency by removing the necessity for further activity."

"Well, that's sound enough," I acquiesced; "but I shall hear from you, I hope?"

"Of course, my dear fellow," he laughed, "we're in this thing together. You'll hear from me as often as you want, and who knows what else besides. I have no intention of dropping this for a minute, Ewart. But I think I can do more if I am not on the spot. We're agreed that my presence here may be a source of danger to you all."

"Yes," I said, "I think yours is the best plan. What do you propose to do?"

"Well, to begin with, I shall devote an hour or two to knocking our panic theory on the head."

"You mean the natural phenomenon idea?"

"Precisely," said he. "I don't think that it will be able to exist very long in the light of physical knowledge—not that that is a very powerful light, but it should be strong enough for our purpose. As soon as I have convinced myself that our enemy is a mere human being I shall take such steps as I may think necessary at the time. Then, of course, I shall acquaint you with the steps that I have taken, and we shall work together and round up our man, and, figuratively speaking, make him swallow his hideous green ray."

"What sort of steps do you mean?" I asked.

"Well, that all depends," my friend answered, "on what sort of man we have to deal with. But it will certainly include providing ourselves with the necessary means of self-defence, and may run to calling in the assistance of the authorities."

"I'm not sure that the presence of the police in a quiet spot like this might not have a disastrous effect on our plans," I pointed out.

"I shouldn't worry about the police," he laughed. "I should make for the naval chaps. I'm rather pally with them just now; I'm booked up to do some work of various descriptions for the period of the war, and I think if I can give them the promise of a little fun and excitement they would be willing to help."

"Which indeed they could," I agreed readily. "Any attempt our enemy might make to get away from us would probably mean a bolt for the open sea, and a few dozen dreadnoughts would be cheerful companionship."

Garnesk laughed, and we strolled up to the house, putting the finishing touches to our toilet as we went. Shortly after breakfast we made ready for our trip to Mallaig. Myra was very anxious to come with us until I explained that we should have to wait there till we had met Dennis and seen the specialist off. She was naturally sensitive about appearing in public with the shade on, poor child, so she readily gave up the idea.

"I'm very sorry you're going, Mr. Garnesk," said Myra, as she shook hands.

"I shall see you again soon," he replied. "I have by no means finished with your case, and as soon as you report the effect of the glasses I shall send you'll see me come tripping in one afternoon, or else I shall ask you to come down to me."

"It's very good of you to take so much trouble about it," said Myra gratefully.

"Not at all," he responded lightly. "It is a pleasure, Miss McLeod, I assure you."

The old general was still more effusive of his gratitude, and as he waved good-bye from the landing-stage his face was almost comically eloquent of regret.

"By the way," said Garnesk as we passed Glasnabinnie, "don't tell Hilderman much about what has happened. We feel we can trust him, but you never know a man's propensity for talking until you know him very well."

"Right," I agreed. "I'll take care of that. We can't afford to get this talked about. It would be very painful for Myra and her father if it became the chatter of the country-side."

"Besides," Garnesk pointed out, "it will be much safer to be quiet about it. If we are dealing with men they will probably prove to be desperate men, and we don't want to run any risks that we can avoid."

"No," said I, "this is going to be quite unpleasant enough without looking for trouble."

So when we arrived in Mallaig and met Hilderman on the fish-table I was careful to remember my companion's advice.

"Ah, Mr. Ewart!" the American exclaimed in surprise, "How are you? And you, Professor? I hope your visit has proved entirely satisfactory. How is Miss McLeod?"

"Just the same, I am sorry to say," Garnesk replied glibly. "There is no sign at all of her sight returning. I can make nothing of it whatever."

"Dear, dear, Professor!" Hilderman exclaimed, with a shake of the head. "That is very bad, very bad indeed. Haven't you even any idea as to how the poor young lady lost her sight?"

"None whatever," said Garnesk, with a hopeless little shrug. "I can't imagine anything, and I'm not above admitting that I know nothing. There is no use my pretending I can do anything for poor Miss McLeod when I feel convinced that I can't."

"So you've given it up altogether, Mr. Garnesk?" Hilderman asked, as we strolled to the station.

"What else can I do?" the oculist replied. "I can't stop up here for ever, much as I should prefer to stay until I had done something for my patient."

"You have my sympathy, Mr. Ewart," said Hilderman in a friendly voice. "It is a terrible blow for you all. I fervently hope that something may yet be done for the poor young lady."

"I hope so too," I answered, with a heavy sigh, but the sigh was merely a convincing response to the lead Garnesk had given me, for, as a matter of fact, I was quite certain that we had found the basis of complete cure.

"Yes," Hilderman muttered, as if thinking aloud, "it is a very terrible and strange affair altogether. Have you had any news about the dog?"

"None whatever," I replied, this time with perfect truth.

"Surely you must suspect somebody, though," the American urged. "It is a very sparsely populated neighbourhood, you know."

"We can't actually suspect anybody, nevertheless," said I. "On the one hand, it may have been an ordinary, uninteresting thief who stole the dog with a view to selling him again. On the other hand——"

"Well," said Hilderman with interest, as I paused, "on the other hand?"

"It may have been someone who had other reasons for stealing him," I concluded.

"I don't quite follow you."

"Ewart means," said Garnesk, cutting in eagerly, evidently fearing that I was about to make some indiscreet disclosure of our suspicions, though I had not the slightest intention of doing so, "Ewart means that it may have been someone who regarded the dog as a personal enemy. Miss McLeod informs us that there was a man in the hills, ostensibly a crofter, who disliked Sholto, quite unreasonably. He drove the dog away from his croft and was very rude to Miss McLeod about it. She suspected an illicit still, and thought the fellow was afraid Sholto might nose out his secret and give the show away."

"Ah!" said Hilderman. "An illicit still, eh! Where was this still, or, rather, where was the croft?"

I remembered that Myra had told us it was somewhere up Suardalan way, above Tor Beag, and I was just about to explain, when I felt my friend's boot knock sharply against my ankle. Taking this as a hint and not an accident, I promptly lied.

"It was miles away," I announced readily, "away up on The Saddle. Miss McLeod wanders pretty far afield with Sholto at times."

"Indeed," said the American, "I should think that might be quite a likely explanation, and rather a suitable place for a still, too. I climbed The Saddle some months ago with an enthusiastic friend of mine. We went by water to Invershiel, and then drove up the Glen. I shouldn't like to walk from Invermalluch and back; there are several mountains in between, and surely there is no road."

Evidently our shrewd companion suspected that I had either made a mistake or deliberately told him an untruth, but I was quite ready for him. I had no time to consider the ethics of the matter. I was out to obey what I took to be my instructions, and obey them I did.

"Oh, there are quite a lot of ways of getting there," I replied airily; "but perhaps the easiest would be to take the motor-boat to Corran and walk up the Arnisdale, or follow the road to Corran and then up the river. Miss McLeod has her own ways of getting about this country, though, and she may even know some way of avoiding the difficulties of the Sgriol and the other intervening mountains."

Hilderman looked at me in considerable surprise for a moment.

"You seem to know the district pretty well yourself, Mr. Ewart," he remarked.

"Well, I ought to," I explained; "I was born in Glenmore."

"Oh, I didn't know that," he murmured; "that accounts for it, then." And at that moment we heard the train approaching, and we hurried into the station to meet our respective visitors.

"Fact or fancy?" asked Garnesk in an undertone as we strolled down the platform, Hilderman having hurried on ahead.

"Fancy," I replied. "I took it you wanted me to avoid giving him the precise details."

"Yes, I did," he laughed. "But you certainly made them precise enough. It is better to be careful how you explain these things to strangers."

"Why?" I asked. "If we suspected Hilderman I should be inclined to agree with you that we should feed him up with lies; and if you think it will help us at all to suspect him I'm on at once. But as we both feel that his disposition is friendly and that we have no cause to doubt him, what is your reason for putting him off the scent every time? I know you well enough by this time to feel sure that you haven't been making these cryptic remarks for the sake of hearing yourself speak."

"Here's the train," he said. "I'll tell you later."

I looked along the carriages for Dennis, but I had evidently missed him, for as I turned back along the platform I found him looking round for me, standing amid the *melee* of tourists and fisherfolk, keepers and valets, sportsmen and dogs, which is typical of the West Highland terminus in early August, and which seemed little affected by the fact that a state of war existed between Great Britain and the only nation in the world which was prepared for hostilities.

"Well, old man," I greeted him as we shook hands heartily. "You got my wire, of course. I hope you had a decent journey."

"Rather, old chap, I should think I did!" he replied warmly. "Slept like a turnip through the beastly parts, and woke up for the bit from Dumbarton on. I also had the luck to remember what you said about the breakfast and took the precaution of wiring for it. Here I am, and as fit as a fiddle."

"That's great!" I exclaimed cheerily, for Dennis's bright attitude had exactly the effect on me that it was intended to have—it made me feel about twenty years younger. "This is Mr. Garnesk, the specialist, who very kindly came from Glasgow to see Myra. Mr. Garnesk—Mr. Burnham."

The two shook hands, and the oculist suggested lunch. We left the station to go up to the hotel, but we saw Hilderman and his newly arrived friend—the same man who had seen me taking Myra up to London—walking leisurely up the hill in front of us. Garnesk took my arm.

"Steady, my boy, steady," he said quietly. "We don't want to be overheard giving the lie to your dainty conversation of a few minutes ago. Isn't there anywhere else we can lunch, because they are evidently on the same tack?"

"Yes," I replied, turning back, "there's the Marine just behind you. That'll do us well. Then we can come out and talk freely where there's no chance of our being overheard."

So we lunched at the Marine Hotel, after which we strolled round the harbour, along the most appalling "road" in the history of civilisation, popularly and well named "the Kyber." Safely out of earshot, I made a hurried mental *precis* of the events

of the past few days, and gave Dennis the resultant
summary as tersely as I could.

"I'm very glad you had Mr. Garnesk with you,"
said Dennis at last, with a glance of frank
admiration at the young specialist.

"Not so glad as I am," I replied fervently. "What I
should have done without him heaven only knows. I
can't even guess."

"Oh, nonsense!" cried Garnesk, in modest protest.
"I haven't been able to do anything. Our one advance
was a piece of pure luck—the discovery that Miss
McLeod could see by the light of a red lamp. We have
decided to keep that quite to ourselves, Mr.
Burnham."

"Of course," agreed Dennis, so emphatically that I
laughed.

"Why so decided, Den?" I asked, for I felt that I
should like to climb to the topmost pinnacle of the
highest peak in all the world and shout the good
news to the four corners of the earth.

"I'm not a scientist, Ron," Dennis replied. "That
may account for the heresy of my profound disbelief
in science. I wouldn't cross the road to see a 'miracle.'
The twentieth century is uncongenial to anything of
that sort. Take it from me, old chap, there's a man at
the back of this—not a nice man, I admit, but an
ordinary human being to all outward appearances—
and when we catch a glimpse of his outward
appearances we shall know what to do."

"Yes, *when* we do," I sighed.

"You mustn't let Ewart get depressed about
things, Mr. Burnham. He very naturally looks at this
business from a different standpoint. With him it is
a tragic, mysterious horror, which threatens the

well-being, if not the existence, of a life that is dearer to him than his own."

"I'll look after him," said Dennis, with a grim determination which made even Garnesk laugh.

"When you two precious people have finished nursing me," I said, "I hope you'll allow me to point out that that very reason gives me a prior claim to take any risks or run into any dangers that may crop up from now on. If there is any trouble brewing, particularly dangerous trouble, then it is my place to tackle it. I am deeply grateful to you fellows for all you have done and are doing and intend to do, but the nursing comes from the other side. I can't let you run risks in a cause which is more mine in the nature of things than yours."

"I fancy," said Dennis, "that even your eloquent speeches will have very little effect when it comes to real trouble. If danger comes it'll come suddenly, and we shall be best helping our common cause by looking after ourselves."

"Hear, hear," said Garnesk, and I could only mutter my thanks and my gratitude for the possession of two staunch friends.

"To get back to business," I said presently, "why did you want me to bluff Hilderman like that?"

"Because," said Garnesk slowly, "I'm not sure that Hilderman is the man to take into our confidence too completely. It's not that I don't trust the man, but he looks so alert and so cute, and has such a dreamy way of pretending he isn't listening to you when you know jolly well that he is, that I have a feeling we ought to be careful with him."

"Very much what Dennis said about him the first time he saw him. But if you don't suspect him, and he is a very cute man, why not trust him and have the benefit of his intelligence?"

"How would you answer that question yourself, Ewart?" the specialist asked quietly.

"Oh," I laughed, "I should point out that his cuteness may be the very reason that we don't suspect him."

"Precisely," Garnesk agreed; "and that is partly my answer as well."

"And the other part?" put in Dennis quietly.

"Well, it's a difficult thing to say, and it's all conjecture. But I have a feeling that Hilderman is not what he says he is. He has a knack of doing things, a way of going about here, that gives me the impression he is employing his intelligence, and a very fine intelligence it probably is, all the time. I don't think he is retired at all. There's a restless energy about the fellow that would turn into a sour discontent if his mind were not fully occupied with work which it is accustomed to, and probably enjoys doing."

"Have you anything to suggest?" I asked.

"I have an idea," he replied; "but I haven't mentioned it because it doesn't satisfy me at all. I have an idea that the man is some sort of detective hard at work all the time. But I can't imagine what sort of detective would take a house up here and keep himself as busy as Hilderman appears to be over some case in the neighbourhood. I can't imagine what sort of case it can be."

"What about a secret German naval base in the Hebrides?" I suggested. "It's not by any means impossible or even unlikely that the Germans have utilised the lonely lochs and creeks to some sinister purpose. Many of the lochs are entirely hidden by surrounding mountains, which come right down to the edge of a narrow opening, and make the place almost unnoticeable unless you happen to be looking for it."

"There's something in that, certainly," Garnesk agreed; "but we must remember he's been here since May. Surely our precious Government would have managed to find what they wanted, and clear it out by this time. Then again, did they suspect the base, or did they have a general idea that war was coming so far back as May?"

"As to the war," Dennis put in, "we don't really know when the authorities had their first suspicions."

"No," said I; "but I fancy it was not a very definite suspicion until after the Archduke was assassinated. But look here, Garnesk, just let us suppose Hilderman really is a Government detective in the guise of an American visitor. Wouldn't he be just about the man we want, or do you think it would make too much stir to take him into our confidence?"

"Far too much," Garnesk replied emphatically. "It's not that he would talk; but if he has been here all this time his opponents have got wind of him long before this, and his arrival on the scene in connection with our case would give any suspicious character the tip to bolt. I should advise keeping in touch with Hilderman, learn as much as you can about him, and be ready to run to him for help if you come to the conclusion that he is the man to give it."

We sat down among the heather at the foot of the Mallaig Vec road, and looked out over the harbour.

"Don't turn your heads," said Dennis quietly, "but glance down at the pier."

"Yes," said Garnesk in a moment, "he seems to be as interested in us as we are in him."

Hilderman and his friend were standing on the end of the pier watching us through their field-glasses.

CHAPTER XIII. THE RED-HAIRED MAN

"I'll send the glasses at once," said Garnesk, as the train steamed out of the station. Dennis and I stood on the platform and watched him out of sight.

"He seems a good fellow," said Dennis.

"Splendid!" I agreed readily. "He's exceeding clever and wide-awake, and very charming. What we should have done without him heaven only knows. I fancy his visit saved the entire household from a nervous collapse."

"We've no time for collapses, nervous or otherwise," Dennis replied. "We shall want our wits about us, and we shall need all the vitality we can muster. But at the same time I don't think there is any cause for nerves. You're not the sort of man, Ron, to let your nerves get the better of you in an emergency, especially if we can prove that our enemy is a tangible quantity, and not a conglomeration of waves and vibrations."

"Hilderman and his friend appear to be waiting for us," I interrupted.

"You may as well introduce me," said Dennis. "I'd like to meet the man. Who is his friend, do you know?"

"Haven't the remotest idea," I replied. "I have seen him once before, but that is all. I don't know who he is."

"Is he staying with Hilderman, or does he live in the neighbourhood?"

"That I couldn't tell you either," I said. "I'm sure he doesn't live anywhere near Invermalluch."

As we strolled out of the station Hilderman and his companion were standing chatting by the gate which leads on to the pier. As we approached, Hilderman turned to me with a smile.

"Ah, Mr. Ewart," he exclaimed, "your friend has left you, then. I hope you won't let his inability to help Miss McLeod depress you unduly. While there's life there's hope."

"I shall not give up hope yet awhile, anyway," I answered heartily.

"May I introduce my friend Mr. Fuller?" he asked presently, and I found myself shaking hands with the round-faced little man, who blinked at me pleasantly through his glasses. I returned the compliment by introducing Dennis.

"On holiday, Mr. Burnham?" asked the American. Dennis was so prompt with his reply that I was convinced he had been thinking it out in the meanwhile.

"Well, I hardly know that I should call it a holiday," he replied immediately. "I have just run up to say good-bye to Ewart before offering my services to my King and country. We had intended to join up together, but he has, as you know, been detained for the time being, so I am off by myself."

"We are very old friends," I explained, "and Burnham very decently decided to come here to see me as I was unable to go south to see him."

"Never mind, Mr. Ewart," said Hilderman. "I guess you'll be able to join him very soon. I wish you luck, Mr. Burnham. I suppose it won't be long before you leave."

"He's talking of returning to-morrow," I cut in. "I wish you'd tell him it's ridiculous, Mr. Hilderman. Fancy coming all this way for twenty-four hours. He must have a look round, to say nothing of his stinginess in depriving me of his company so soon."

"Well, I can quite understand Mr. Burnham's anxiety to join at the earliest possible moment," he answered. "But I've no doubt Lord Kitchener wouldn't miss him for a day. I think he might multiply his visit by two, and stop till Wednesday, at any rate. Ah, here's the *Fiona!*"

I looked out to the mouth of the harbour, and saw the steam yacht, which was in the habit of calling at Glasnabinnie, gliding past the lighthouse rock. I was about to make some comment on the boat when Hilderman forestalled me.

"How are you going back?" he asked.

"In a motor-boat," I replied. "I am afraid Angus is getting weary of waiting already."

"I'm sure Mr. Fuller would be delighted to have you fellows on board. Why not let your man take Mr. Burnham's luggage to Invermalluch, and come to Glasnabinnie on the *Fiona*? You can lunch with me, and when you tire of our company I will run you across in the *Baltimore*. Eh? What do you say?"

"I shall be delighted, of course," his companion broke in.

I hesitated for a moment, and glanced at Dennis. His face obviously said, "Accept," so I accepted.

"Thank you," I said; "we shall be very pleased. It will be more jolly than going back by ourselves."

"Good!" cried Hilderman, "and I can show you the view from my smoking-room. I hope it will make you green with envy."

So I gave Angus his instructions, and the four of us waited at the fish-table steps for the dinghy to come ashore from the yacht. She was not a particularly beautiful boat, but she looked comfortable and strong, and her clumsy appearance was accentuated by the fact that her funnel was aft a commodious deck dining-saloon, on the top of which was a small wheel-house. Myra had been right, as it turned out; she was a converted drifter. The two men who came in to pick us up wore the usual blue guernsey, with *S.Y. Fiona* worked in an arc of red wool across the chest. They were obviously good servants and useful hands, but there was none of that ridiculous imitation of naval custom and etiquette which delights the heart of the Cotton Exchange yacht-owner. We boarded the *Fiona* with the feeling that we were going to have a pleasant and comfortable time, and not with the fear that our setting of a leather-soled shoe upon the hallowed decks was in itself an act of sacrilege. We were no sooner aboard than Fuller set himself to play the host with a charm which was exceedingly attentive and neither fussy nor patronising.

"The trivial but necessary question of edible stores will detain us for a few moments," he said. "But we shall be more comfortable here than wandering about among the herrings." So we made ourselves comfortable in deck-chairs in the stern, while the steward went ashore and made the all-important purchases.

"You cruise a good deal, I suppose?" was my first question.

"Yes, a fair amount," our host replied. "I pretty well live on board, you know, although I have a small house further north, on Loch Duich, if you know where that is."

"Mr. Ewart was born up here, and knows it backwards," Hilderman informed him. And we chatted about the district and the fishing and the views until the steward returned, and we got under weigh. I should have liked to have seen the accommodation below, but the journey was a short one, and I had no opportunity to make the suggestion. Dennis was sitting nearest the rail, and there was a small hank of rope at his feet.

"I beg your pardon, Mr. Burnham," said Fuller suddenly. "I didn't notice that rope was in your way." And he learned over and tossed the rope away. As he did so some hard object fell with a clatter from the coil.

"It's not interfering with me in the least," laughed Dennis, and looked down at a large, bone-handled clasp-knife which had dropped in front of him. He picked it up idly, and weighed it in his hand.

"Useful sort of implement," he said.

"Oh, these sailor-chaps like a big knife more than anything," said Hilderman; "and, of course, they need them strong. I daresay that has been used for anything, from primitive carpentry to cutting tobacco. The one knife always does for everything."

We continued our conversation while Dennis idly examined the knife, opening it and studying the blade absently. Presently Fuller, noticing his absorption, began to chaff him about it.

"Well," he laughed, "have you compiled a complete history of the knife and it's owner? If you're ready to sit an examination on the subject I will constitute myself examiner, then we'll find who the knife belongs to, and corroborate or contradict your conclusions."

"It's a very ordinary knife to find on board a boat, I should think," said Dennis.

"Oh come, Mr. Burnham," Hilderman joined in, "you mustn't wriggle out of it. Surely you can answer Mr. Fuller's questions."

"If Mr. Fuller will allow me to put one or two preliminary questions to him," Dennis replied, entering into the spirit of fun, "I am ready to go into the witness-box and swear quite a number of fanciful things."

"Come now, Fuller," chaffed Hilderman. "You must give him a run for his money, you know. He is risking his reputation at a moment's notice. I think you ought to let him ask you three questions, at any rate."

"Fire away, Mr. Burnham," said our host. "I'll give you a start of three questions, and then you must be prepared to answer every reasonable question I put to you, or be branded publicly as an unreliable witness and an incompetent detective."

Dennis puffed at his pipe and smiled, and I was surprised to see that he really was bringing his mind to bear on the trivial problem with all the acuteness he had in him.

"Well, in the first place," he asked, "do you stop in port very often overnight, or for any length of time during the day?"

"I never stop in port longer than I can help," laughed Fuller, "or the owner of that knife would probably take the opportunity of buying a new one, and throwing this old thing away. All the same, I don't see how that is going to help you."

"Ah," said Dennis, in bantering vein, "you mustn't expect me to give away my process, you know. The secret's been in the family for years."

"What's your second question, Den?" I asked.

"Is there a hotel within reasonable distance of your house on Loch Whatever-it-is, Mr. Fuller?"

"Loch Duich?" our host replied. "There's one about six miles by road and eleven or twelve by the sea."

"I don't think I need ask you the third question, then," said Dennis. "You can begin your examination now."

"Now, Mr. Burnham," Fuller commenced, "you quite understand that anything you say will be taken down in writing, and may be used as evidence against you?"

"I assure you I have a keen appreciation of the gravity of the situation," Dennis replied seriously.

"Well," said Fuller, "I'll begin with an easy one— one that won't tax your powers of observation beyond endurance."

"Yes," I urged, "let him down gently. He does his best."

"What profession does the owner of that knife follow?"

Hilderman and I laughed.

"We may as well count that answer as read," he said.

"There's a catch there, Dennis," I warned him. "The legal designation is 'mariner.'"

"I don't think it is," said my friend.

"We won't quarrel about terms," laughed our host graciously. "Sailor or seaman or deckhand will do just as well."

"No," said Dennis, "it won't. The owner of this knife is not a sailor by profession."

"But," Fuller protested, "it must belong to one of my crew, and it is obviously a seaman's knife."

"In that case," Dennis answered, "I think you'll find that you have a man on board who is not a professional seaman in the ordinary use of the term. I'll tell you what I think of this knife, shall I?"

"By all means," urged Hilderman and his friend together, and I began to take a keen interest in this curious discussion, for I could see that Dennis was no longer playing. He turned the knife over in his hand, and looked up at Fuller.

"Mr. Fuller," he said quietly, "the owner of this knife is not a sailor by profession. He is probably a schoolmaster. I can't be sure of that, but I can say this definitely: he is a professional man of some sort, possibly an engineer, but, as I say, more probably a mathematical master. He is left-handed, has red hair, a wife, and at least one child."

I shouted with laughter when I realised how thoroughly my friend had pulled my leg, but I broke off abruptly when Hilderman sat bolt upright, and his chair and Fuller's cigar fell unheeded on to the deck. But in a second they took their cue from me, and roared with laughter.

"Oh, excellent, Mr. Burnham," said Hilderman between his guffaws. "But you forgot to mention that his sister married a butcher's assistant."

"Ah, but I don't admit she did," Dennis protested.

"I'm very much indebted to you for exposing this masquerader," said Fuller. "I shall have the matter inquired into. But seriously, Mr. Burnham, you made one extraordinary fluke in your deductions, which almost took my breath away. I have a man on board with red hair, and when the boat came into the harbour he was working about here. I saw him leave his work to come ashore for us. I shouldn't be at all surprised to find that the knife belonged to him."

"Oh, well," Dennis laughed, "one shot right is not a bad average for a beginner, you know."

"No," said Hilderman, puffing a cloud of smoke, and dreamily following its ascent with his eyes, "not bad at all. Not bad at all."

And then, the joke of the clasp-knife being played out, we admired the scenery, and conversed of less speculative subjects till we arrived at Glasnabinnie.

We were pulled ashore by the man with the red hair, and when our host confronted him with the knife he promptly claimed it.

"I think you won, Mr. Burnham," laughed Fuller, and Dennis smiled in reply. We slid alongside the landing-stage and stepped out, and Dennis's schoolmaster was about to slip the painter through a ring and make the boat fast. But evidently the ring was broken. The man came ashore, and Hilderman began to lead us up the path. But Dennis deliberately turned and watched the sailor. Hilderman and his companion strolled ahead while I stood beside Dennis. The man with the red hair fished among a pile of wire rope, and picked out a small marline-spike. Then he lifted a large stone, held the marline-spike on the wooden planking of the landing-stage, and hammered it in with the stone. Then he threw the painter round it, and made the boat secure in that way.

"Yes," murmured Dennis quietly, as we turned to join the others, "I think I won."

For the man had held the stone in his left hand.

CHAPTER XIV. A FURTHER MYSTERY

"Well," said Hilderman, as we caught them up, "what about lunch? After his journey I daresay Mr. Burnham has an appetite, not to mention his excursion into the realm of detective fiction."

"We lunched at Mallaig," I explained, "with Mr. Garnesk before we saw him off."

"Oh, did you?" he asked, with evident surprise. "I didn't see you at the hotel."

"We went to the Marine," I replied, "to save ourselves a climb up the hill."

"We had a snack at Mallaig too," the American continued, "intending to lunch here. Are you sure you couldn't manage something?"

"It would have to be a very slight something," Dennis put in. "But I daresay we could manage that."

"Good!" said Hilderman. "Come along, then, and let's see what we can do."

We strolled into the drawing-room through the inevitable verandah, and though Hilderman was the tenant of the furnished house he had contrived to impart a suggestion of his own personality to the room. The furniture was arranged in a delightfully lazy manner that almost made you yawn. The walls were hung with photographic enlargements of some of the most beautiful spots in the neighbourhood. I remembered what Myra had told me as to his being an enthusiastic photographer, so I asked him about them.

"Did you take these, Mr. Hilderman?"

"Yes," he answered. "These are just a few of the best. I have many others which I should like you to see some time. I always leave the enlarging to keep me alive during the winter months. These are a few odd ones I enlarged for decorative purposes."

"They are beautiful," I said enthusiastically, for they were real beauties, more like drawings in monochrome than photographs. "And you certainly seem to have got about the neighbourhood since your arrival."

"Yes," he laughed, "I don't miss much when I get out with my camera. Most of these were taken during the first month of my stay here."

"These snow scenes from the Cuchulins are simply gorgeous, and surely this is the Kingie Pool on the Garry?"

"Right first time," he admitted, evidently pleased to see his work admired. I thought of Garnesk's suspicion that our American friend was engaged on detective work of some kind, and it struck me that with his camera and his obvious talent he had an excellent excuse for going almost anywhere, supposing he were called upon at any time to explain his presence in some outlandish spot.

"You must have kept yourself exceedingly busy," I remarked in conclusion.

After the meal we adjourned to the hut above the falls. Hilderman certainly had some right to be proud of his view. It was magnificent. We stood outside the door and gazed out to sea, north, south and west, for some minutes.

"You have the same uninterrupted view from inside," said Hilderman, as we mounted the three steps to the door. He held the door open, and I stepped in first, followed by Dennis and Fuller. The window extended the whole length of the room, and folded inwards and upwards, in the same way as some greenhouse windows do. Suddenly I laughed aloud.

"What's the joke?" asked Hilderman.

"This," I said, pointing to a large carbon transparency of a mountain under snow, which hung in the window on the north side. "You've no idea how this has been annoying us over at Invermalluch."

"How?" asked Dennis.

"It swings about in the breeze," I replied, "and it reflects the light and catches everybody's eye. It's a very beautiful photograph, Mr. Hilderman, but, like many human beings, it's exceedingly unpopular owing to the position it holds."

"A thousand apologies, Mr. Ewart," said the American. "It shall be removed at once."

"Oh, not at all!" I protested. "Surely you are entitled to hang a positive of a photograph in your window without receiving a protest from neighbours who live nearly three miles away."

"That's Invermalluch Lodge, then, across the water," Dennis asked.

"Yes," I replied, and we forgot about the transparency, which remained in undisputed possession of a pitch to which it was certainly entitled. We sat and smoked, and looked out at the mountains of Skye and the wonderful panorama of sea and loch, with an occasional glance at the gurgling waterfall at our feet, and presently I picked up a copy of an illustrated paper which was lying at my hand. I turned the pages idly, and threw a cursory glance at the photographs of the week's brides, and the latest efforts of the theatrical press agents, and I noticed, without thinking anything of the fact, that one page had been roughly torn out. I was about to remark that probably the most interesting or amusing picture in the whole paper had been accidentally destroyed, when Fuller leaned across Dennis, and took the paper out of my hands.

"Don't insult Mr. Hilderman's precious view by reading the paper in his smoking-room, Mr Ewart," he said, with a loud laugh. "As a Highlander you should have more tact than that."

Hilderman turned round, and looked from one to other of us.

"What paper is he reading? I didn't know there was one here."

I explained what paper it was, adding, "I quite admit that it was a waste of time when I ought to be admiring your unrivalled view, Mr. Hilderman. I offer you my sincere apologies."

Hilderman threw a quick glance at Mr. Fuller.

"Better give it him back, Fuller," he said. "There is nothing more annoying than to have a paper snatched away from you when you're half-way through it."

Shortly after that Fuller declared that he must be leaving, and asked Hilderman rather pointedly whether he felt like a trip to Loch Duich. I determined to step in with an idea of my own.

"I was going to make a suggestion myself, Mr. Hilderman," I began, "but it doesn't matter if you are engaged."

"Well, I don't know that I'm particularly keen to come with you this afternoon, Fuller," he remarked. "What was your suggestion, Mr. Ewart?"

"I was wondering whether you would come over to Invermalluch with Burnham and me and—er—have a look round with us?"

"Well, if Fuller doesn't think it exceedingly rude of me, I should like to," the American replied, "especially as Mr. Burnham will be leaving you to-morrow, or the day after at latest."

"Incidentally, I don't know how we shall get back without you," I pointed out. "You see, we sent the motor-boat on."

"By Jove, so you did!" Hilderman exclaimed. "Well, that settles it, Fuller."

"I could take them on the *Fiona* and put them ashore," his companion persisted. Hilderman gave Fuller a look which seemed to clinch the matter, however, for the little man beamed at me through his spectacles, and explained that if he took us in his yacht it would be killing two birds with one stone.

"Still, of course, my dear fellow," he concluded, "you must please yourselves entirely."

So we saw him safely on board the *Fiona*, and then started for Invermalluch in Hilderman's magnificent Wolseley launch.

"Fuller knows me," he explained, by way of apology. "I go up with him sometimes as often as three times a week, but I gathered that you asked me with a view to discussing the mystery of the green flash, or whatever you call it."

"You're quite right; I did," I replied. "I simply want you to come and have a look at the river, and see what you can make of it."

"Anything I can do, you know, Mr. Ewart," he assured me, "I shall be delighted to do. If you think it will be of any assistance to you if I explore the river with you—well, I'm ready now."

From that we proceeded to give him, at his request, minute details of Garnesk's conclusions on the matter, and I am afraid I departed from the truth with a ready abandon and a certain relish of which I ought to have been most heartily ashamed.

When we stepped ashore at Invermalluch Hilderman looked back across the water.

"If I'd waited for Fuller," he laughed, "I should have been stuck there yet. He's let the water go off the boil or something."

We went up to the house and had tea on the verandah, for the General had taken Myra up Loch Hourn in the motor-boat. After tea we got to business.

"Now that I've had a very refreshing cup of tea," the American remarked, "I feel rather like the mouse who said '*Now* bring out your cat' when he had consumed half a teaspoonful of beer! Now show me the river."

"I don't want to sound at all panicky," I said, "but I think I ought to warn you that our experiences at the particular spot we are going to have—well, shall we say they have provided a striking contrast from the routine of our daily life?"

"I'm not at all afraid of the river, Mr. Ewart," he replied lightly. "I should be the last person to doubt the statements of yourself and Miss McLeod and the General, but I am inclined to think the river has no active part in the proceedings."

"You hold the view that it was the merest coincidence that Miss McLeod and the General both had terrible and strange experiences at the same spot?" asked Dennis.

"It seems to be the only sensible view to hold," Hilderman declared emphatically. "I must say I think Miss McLeod's blindness might have happened in her own room or anywhere else, and the General's strange experience seems to me to be the delusion of overwrought nerves. I confess there is only one thing I don't understand, and that is the disappearance of the dog. That's got me beaten, unless it was that crofter."

"We intend to go to the Saddle to-morrow and make a few investigations. I was going by myself," I added cautiously, "but I think I can persuade Burnham to stay and go with me."

"I certainly should stay for that, Mr. Burnham," Hilderman advised. "One more day can't make much difference."

"I'll think it over," said Dennis, careful not to commit himself rashly.

We came to the Dead Man's Pool, and crossed over the river, and began to walk up the other side.

"This is about the right time for a manifestation of the mystery," I remarked lightly, though I was far from laughing about the whole thing.

"Well," said Hilderman, "if we are to see the green flash in operation I hope it will be in a gentle mood, and not pull our teeth out one by one or anything of that sort." Evidently he had little sympathy with our fear of the green ray and the awe with which we approached the neighbourhood of the river.

"Are we going to the right place?" Dennis asked. "I mean the identical spot?"

"That lozenge-shaped thing up there is the Chemist's Rock," I replied, "and the other important place is Dead Man's Pool, which we have just left."

"Miss McLeod went blind on the Chemist's Rock, didn't she?" Dennis inquired.

"Yes," I replied, with a shudder. "She was fishing from it."

"Then suppose we go back to the pool," he suggested. We agreed readily enough, for I had no desire to hang about the fateful rock, and Hilderman for his part seemed to have no faith in the idea at all. I fancy he thought it would make no difference to us in what part of the river we might be, only provided we didn't fall in. So Dennis led the way back, and he was the first to pick his way to the middle of the stream. Hilderman and I were some distance behind. Suddenly we stopped stock-still, and looked at him. He had begun to cough and splutter, and he seemed rooted to the small stone he was standing on in the middle of the stream. In a flash I understood, and with a cry I bounded after him, Hilderman following at my heels.

"It's all right, Ewart," cried Hilderman behind me. "He's only choked, or something of that sort. He'll be all right in a minute."

Dennis had crossed to the centre of the stream by a way of his own, and we ran down to the stepping-stones by which we had come, in order to save the time which we should have been compelled to waste in feeling for a foothold as we went. Every second was of importance, and I fully expected to see Dennis topple unconscious into the pool below before I should be able to save him. I knew what it was exactly; he was going through my own horrible experience of "drowning on dry land," to quote Garnesk's vigorous phrase. Imagine my astonishment, therefore, when I reached Dennis's side with only a slight difficulty in breathing. There was no sign, or at least very little, of the air which was "heavier than water." Hilderman plunged along behind me, and we reached the stone on which my friend was standing almost simultaneously. Dennis held an arm pointing up the river, his face transfixed with an expression of horrified amazement. Suddenly Hilderman gave a hoarse, shrill shout, breaking almost into a scream.

"Shut your eyes!" he yelled. "Shut your eyes! Oh, for heaven's sake, shut your eyes!"

But I never thought of following his advice. Dennis's immovable arm, pointing like an inanimate signpost up the river, fascinated me. Slowly I raised my eyes in that direction. Then I stepped back with a startled cry, lost my footing, slipped, and fell on my face among the rocks.

The river had disappeared!

CHAPTER XV. CONCERNS AN ILLUSTRATED PAPER

The river had disappeared!

In front of us was a great green wall of solid rock, which seemed to tower into the sky above us, and to stretch away for miles to right and left. The curious part about it was that the rock was undoubtedly solid. The shrubs that grew upon it, the great crevices and clefts, were all real. I knew—though I had a hard struggle to make myself believe—that it was all a marvellous and indescribable delusion, for there could be no cliff where only a few seconds before there had been a mighty, rushing torrent.

And yet I could have planted finger and foot on the ledges of that solid precipice and climbed to the invisible summit. Hilderman was muttering to himself beneath his breath, but I was too dazed, my brain was too numbed to make any sense out of the confused mumble of words which came from him. Dennis held my arm in a vice-like grip that stopped the circulation, and almost made me cry out with the pain.

Hilderman staggered, his arm over his eyes, across the stepping-stones to the side of the stream. I found my voice at last.

"Dennis!" I shouted at the top of my voice, though why I should have shouted I can never explain, for my friend was standing just beside me. "Dennis, come away, man. Get out of this!"

I exerted my strength to the uttermost, but Dennis was immovable, rooted to the spot by the strange, snake-like fascination of the nightmare. Then, as suddenly as it had arisen, the rock disappeared again, and there before our startled gaze was a peacefully flowing river. Dennis turned to me with a face as white as a sheet.

"The place is haunted," he said, with a somewhat hysterical laugh.

"Let's get away from it and sit down, and think it over," I urged, pulling him away. We made for the side of the river and sat down, at a very safe distance from the bank. I rolled up my sleeve, and had a look at my arm.

"Great Scott!" Dennis exclaimed, as I dangled the pinched and purple limb painfully. "What on earth did that?"

"I'm afraid it was your own delicate touch and dainty caress that did it, old man. You seized hold of me as if you hadn't seen me for years, and I owed you a thousand pounds."

"Ron, my dear fellow," he said penitently, "I'm most awfully sorry. Why didn't you shout?"

I burst out laughing.

"I entered a protest in vigorous terms, but you were otherwise engaged at the moment, and, anyway, don't look so scared about it, old man; it'll be quite all right in a minute."

Poor Dennis was quite upset at the evidence I bore of his absorption in the miracle, and we postponed our discussion while he massaged the injured arm in order to restore the flow of blood.

"Where's Hilderman?" I asked presently, and though we looked everywhere for the American he was nowhere to be seen.

"He didn't look the sort to funk like that," said Dennis thoughtfully.

"I should have been prepared to bet he was quite brave," I concurred. "Well, anyway," I added, "the main point is, what do you think of our entertainment? You've come a long way for it, but I hope you are not disappointed now you've seen it. It's original, isn't it?"

"By heaven, Ron!" he cried, "you're right. It is original. It is even a more unholy, indescribable mystery than I expected, and I never accused you of exaggerating it, even in my own mind."

"I'm glad that both you and Hilderman have had ocular demonstration of it," I remarked. "It is so much more convincing, and will help you to go into the matter without any feeling that we are out on a hare-brained shadow-chase."

"We're certainly not that, anyhow," Dennis agreed emphatically. "It is a real mystery, Ronald, my boy. A real danger, as well, I'm afraid. But we'll stick at it till the end."

"Thanks, old fellow," I said simply, and then I added, "I wonder what can have become of Hilderman?"

"Gad!" cried Dennis, in sudden alarm. "He can't have fallen into the river by any chance?"

We jumped to our feet and looked about us.

"No," I said presently, "he hasn't fallen into the river." And I pointed a finger out to sea. The *Baltimore II.*, churning a frantic way across to

Glasnabinnie, seemed to divide the intervening water in one great white slash.

"I wonder," said Dennis quietly, "*is* that funk, or isn't it?"

We watched the diminishing craft for a minute or two in silence, and finally decided to keep an open mind on the subject until we might have an opportunity to see Hilderman and hear his own explanation.

"Talking about explanations, what about the left-handed schoolmaster with the red-headed wife, or whatever it was?" I asked.

"That was a bit of luck," said Dennis modestly, "and I will admit, if you like, that we owe that to Garnesk."

"Garnesk wasn't there," I protested.

"No," my friend admitted, "he wasn't there at the time, but he put me on the look-out for a left-handed sailor. I was very much impressed with his deductions about the man who stole Miss McLeod's dog, and I determined to be on the look-out for a left-handed man. I also admit that I carefully watched everyone we met, especially the fishermen at Mallaig, to see if I could detect the sort of man I wanted. I was rewarded when we were pulled out to the *Fiona* by those two men of Fuller's. One of them was red-headed, you remember? Well, that man was left-handed. It was very easy to observe that by the way he held his oar and generally handled things. Of course I was very bucked about it, so I paid very close attention to him. He wore a wedding-ring— ergo, he was married. It is not conclusive, of course, but a fairly safe guess when you're playing at toy detectives. So when I found the knife I looked for some sign that it belonged to him, and found it. It was all quite simple."

"I daresay it will be when you explain it, but you haven't in the least explained it yet," I pointed out. "How about the schoolmaster and all that, and what made you think the knife belonged to him."

"Simply because he was very probably—working on the law of averages—the only left-handed man among the crew, and that knife belonged to a left-handed man."

"But my dear old fellow," I cried, "you don't seriously mean to tell me that you can say whether a man is left-handed or not by looking at marks on the handle of his knife?"

"Not on the handle," Dennis explained; "on the blade. Have you got a knife on you?"

I produced my pen-knife.

"I'll trust you with it," I declared confidently. "I've never held any secrets from you, Den."

Dennis opened the knife and laid it in the palm of his hand. I stood still and watched him.

"You've sharpened pencils with this knife and the pencils have left their mark. If you hold the knife as you would when sharpening a pencil and look down on the blade there are no pencil marks visible. Now turn the knife over and you will find the marks on the other side of the blade."

"Half a minute," I said eagerly, "let's have a look. The knife is in position for sharpening a pencil and the back of the knife is pointing to my chest. The marks are underneath." I took a pencil from my pocket and tried it. "Yes, I've got you, Dennis. It's quite clear. If I held the knife with the point to my right instead of to my left, as I should do in sharpening with my left hand, the marks appear on the other side of the blade. It is not quite conclusive, Den, but it's jolly cute."

"Not when you're looking for it," he said. "I was struck by the fact that the knife which, by its size and weight, was a seaman's handy tool, had also been used for the repeated sharpening of a blue pencil. When I saw those indications I went through the motion and came to the conclusion that the marks were on the wrong side. Then I tried with my left hand and accounted for it. The blue pencil made me suspicious. I have no knowledge of a yacht-hand's duties, but surely sharpening blue pencils is not one of them. Then the knife had also been carried in the same pocket as a piece of white chalk. The only sort of person I could think of who would carry a piece of chalk loose in his pocket and use a blue pencil continuously was a schoolmaster. So I stated definitely—there's nothing like bluff—that the knife belonged to the left-handed man, who quite obviously had red hair, who appeared to wear the insignia of the married state, and who—again according to the law of averages—had at least one child. I naturally slumped the schoolmaster idea in with it, and there you have the whole thing in a nutshell. But it was Garnesk who set me looking for left-handed clues, and if I hadn't been looking for it, it would never have entered my head."

"But look here," I suggested, "some people sharpen pencils by pointing the pencil to them. Wouldn't that produce the same effect?"

"Yes," he admitted, "I thought of that. But the marks would have been very much fainter, because there would have been much less pressure. I put that idea aside."

"Good!" I exclaimed. "I should much prefer to swallow your theory whole, Dennis, but it struck me that might be a possible source of error, which, of course, might have led us on to a false trail. And, I say, those questions you asked about the time he stayed in port and the hotel. Were those all bluff? Or had you some sort of idea at the back of them?"

"I had a very definite idea at the back of them," Dennis replied. "I thought perhaps the white chalk which was deposited in the blade-pocket, and was even noticeable on the handle, might be due to billiard chalk. But, of course, I didn't mention billiards, because it would have given my line of reasoning away. I thought it was better to spring it on them with a bump."

"Which you certainly did," I laughed. "As a matter of fact, I thought you were simply having a game with us all. But now that you've told me the details, Den, do you remember what happened when you did spring it on them?"

"Well, of course I do," he replied. "But even so, I hardly know what to make of it. I should like to feel confidently that Fuller is the man we are after. But we must remember that both he and Hilderman might very easily have thought I really had discovered something from the knife and been exceedingly surprised without having any guilty connection with the discovery."

"H'm," I muttered, "I prefer to suspect Fuller."

"Oh, I do too," Dennis agreed. "It is safer to suspect everybody in a case like this. But why are you so emphatic?"

"Well," I explained, "we have a few little things to go on. Myra diagnosed that Sholto was taken on a yacht by Garnesk's left-handed man in sea-boots. Then you produce a left-handed member of a yacht's crew out of an old pocket-knife, and Fuller jumps out of his skin when you mention it. That seems to be something to go on, and then there was that incident in the smoking-room."

"When you were reading the paper?" he asked. "I couldn't make that out. Did you notice anything suspicious about it?"

"Of course I was in a suspicious mood," I admitted, "but it struck me as a singularly rude thing to do to snatch the paper out of my hand like that. His remark about Hilderman's precious view was very weak. I think there was something behind it."

"What?" asked Dennis.

"It may have been that there was a letter, or something in the way of a paper, which he didn't want me to see laid inside the paper; but there was another curious point about it. There was a page torn out. I had just noticed this and was on the point of making some silly remark about it when Fuller leaned right across you and took the thing from me, as you saw."

"If the page he didn't want you to see was torn out, there was no chance of your seeing it," Dennis argued, logically enough.

"No," I agreed, "but after your exhibition, if he had anything to conceal he may have been afraid of my even seeing that the page was torn out."

"What do you imagine the missing page can possibly have contained?"

"I don't know," I answered, and thought hard for a minute. "By Jove, Den!" I cried suddenly, "I believe I've got it. This takes us back to Garnesk's idea of a wireless invention causing all the trouble. We think we have reason to believe that Fuller may have stolen the dog. We also think we have reason to believe that one of his yacht-hands is what you called 'a mathematical master.' Now, suppose the paper had got hold of this and printed an illustration of the mysterious invention or perhaps a photograph of the mysterious inventor?"

"And the inventor, knowing that we should accuse him of blinding Miss McLeod and making off with her dog, the moment we could identify him, tears out the offending illustration in case either we or anyone else in the neighbourhood should see it? He admitted, by the way, that he never went into port if he could help it."

"Well, anyway," I said, "we'll have a look for the paper and find the missing page."

"You noticed the date?" Dennis asked, anxiously.

"Oh! it was this week's issue," I replied.

"Do they take it at the house?" he inquired, again with a note of anxiety.

"Not that I know of, but we'll rake one up somewhere, don't you fret. And, I say, this is a fine way to welcome a visitor; you haven't even said how-do to your host and hostess. I'm most awfully sorry."

"Don't be an ass, Ronnie," said Dennis, cheerfully. "With the utmost respect, as you barrister chaps would say, I hadn't noticed your departure from the requirements of conventional hospitality. I wouldn't have missed this for all the world and a bit of Bond Street."

So then we hurried to the house with a nervous energy, which spoke eloquently to our state of suppressed excitement.

"All the same," Den muttered dolefully, as we hurried down the stable path, "it's going to be what the Americans would call 'some' wireless invention that can plant a grown-up mountain in the middle of an innocent river in the twinkling of an eyelash."

"It is, indeed, old fellow," I agreed, "but don't let us worry about that. We'll get in and see Myra and the General, and then have a look round for the *Pictures*—the paper you were looking at."

We found Myra sitting on the verandah and wondering what on earth had kept us, and if we had changed our minds and gone straight back south with Garnesk.

"I'm most awfully sorry, darling," I apologised. "It's all my fault, of course. We went to Glasnabinnie, and since then I've been showing Dennis the river and generally forgetting my duties as deputy host."

"What did you go to the river for?" Myra asked, suspiciously.

"Oh! just to have a look round, you know, dear. It's a very nice river," I replied, airily.

"Ronnie, dear, please," she said gently, laying her hand on my arm and turning her veiled and shaded face to mine, "please don't joke about it. I can't bear to think of you running risks there."

I looked at my beautiful, blind darling, and a pang shot through me.

"God knows I'm not joking about it, dearest," I said sadly.

"I know you weren't really, Ronnie. But, please, oh! please, keep away from the river."

"Very well, dear," I promised, "I will, unless an urgent duty takes me there. We must solve this mystery somehow, and it may mean my going to the river. But I promise not to run any unnecessary risks."

"I'll keep an eye on him and see that he takes care of himself, Miss McLeod," said Dennis, coming to the rescue.

"Thank you, Mr. Burnham," the girl replied, "but you know it applies to you as well. You must look after yourself also."

"By the way, dear," I asked, changing the subject, "have you a copy of this week's *Pictures*?"

"I'm afraid not," she answered. "Must it be the *Pictures*? I've just been looking at another illustrated paper."

"Looking at what?" I cried, jumping to my feet. "Darling, who's talking about running risks?"

"Oh, it's all right, dear," she assured me. "I got Mary to bring my dark-room lamp down to the den and just glanced at the pictures by the red light. But I won't do it again, if it alarms you, dear. All the same, I'm quite sure I could see by daylight."

"You promised Garnesk you wouldn't till you heard from him, darling," I urged. "It might be very dangerous, so please don't for my sake."

"Very well, then," Myra sighed, "I'll try to be good. But I hope he'll write soon."

"Where do you think we could get a copy of the paper?" I asked shortly.

"If it's frightfully important, dear, you might get one in Glenelg, and, failing that, Doctor Whitehouse would lend you his. I know he takes it in. Why are you so keen about it?"

"We'll go into the den and tell you everything in a minute or two, dear," I promised. "Is there any objection to my sending Angus in to the doctor?"

"None whatever," Myra declared, "he can go now if you like."

So after I had despatched Angus into the village with strict instructions not to come back without a copy of the paper if he valued his life, we all adjourned to Myra's den, and my friend and I told her in detail everything that had happened. About an hour and a half later Angus returned with the paper. I took it from him with a hurried word of thanks and nervously turned over the pages.

"Ah! here's a page I didn't see," I exclaimed excitedly, but the only thing on the whole page was a photograph of a new dancer appearing in London. Without waiting for me to do so, Dennis leaned over me and turned the page over with a quick jerk of the wrist.

"Phew!" I exclaimed involuntarily, and Dennis gave a long, low whistle.

"Oh! what is it? Tell me!" pleaded Myra, anxiously.

"It's a photograph of our friend Fuller," I replied slowly, in a voice that shook with excitement. "And he's wearing court dress, and underneath the photograph are the words 'Baron Hugo von Guernstein, Secretary of the Military Intelligence Department of the Imperial German General Staff.'"

Chapter XVI. Discloses Certain Facts

"There's no doubt about it," I remarked as soon as we had partially recovered from our surprise. "That's Fuller right enough."

"Oh! there's no doubt it's our man," said Dennis emphatically. "Even if we had not the evidence of the torn page to corroborate it, the likeness is perfect."

"Yes," I agreed, "but what do you think his game can be? I'm coming round to Garnesk's wireless theory."

"Whatever it is, we've stumbled on something of real importance this time. We must find out what it is and show it up at once."

"I hope you'll take care," said Myra anxiously. "I shouldn't mind so much if I could be with you to help, but it's dreadful to sit here and know you are in danger and not be able to do anything at all."

"I'm very glad you can't, darling," I said heartily, as I threw my arm round her shoulders. "I don't want you to come rushing into these dangers, whatever they may be. In a way I am glad you are not able to join us, because I know how difficult it would be to stop you if you were."

"I suppose this is all one affair," she said doubtfully. "You don't think this is something quite different from the green ray? It might be two quite separate things, you know."

"I don't think we are likely to meet with two such interesting problems in such a remote locality unless they are connected with each other, Miss McLeod, and especially as everything else apart from the photograph of Baron von Guernstein points to Fuller as the culprit. I think we can take it that in solving one mystery we provide the solution to the other."

"I quite agree with you, Dennis," I said, "but what I am worrying about now is, what we are going to do."

"The first thing you must do is to dress for dinner, and not let anyone imagine there is anything untoward about," Myra advised. "And please don't tell father you have been lunching with one of the Kaiser's principal spies, if that's what the Baron's title really means. I would much rather you said nothing to him at all about it for the present, and in any case you must have something definite in mind as to your plans before you put the matter to him. If you tell him you don't know what to do about it he will be in a dreadful state. He is very far from well, and all this business has told on him dreadfully."

"That is very excellent advice, Miss McLeod," Dennis agreed warmly. "Ronald, we'll go and disguise ourselves as ordinary, undisturbed human beings and hide our fears and doubts behind the breastplate of a starched shirt. Come along."

So Dennis dragged me away, and then, realising his indiscretion, allowed me to return to my *fiancee* "just for two minutes, old fellow."

Dinner was a curious meal, though not quite so strange as the meal the General and I had together the night, less than a week before, that Myra lost her sight.

I hope I shall never live through a week like that again. Even now, as I look back, I cannot believe that it all happened in seven days. It still seems to have been something like seven months at the very least.

We had one thing in our favour as we sat down to the table; we all had a common object in view. We were each of us determined to forget the green ray for a moment. Fortunately the old man took an immediate fancy to Dennis and that brightened me considerably. There are few things so pleasant as to see those whose opinion you value getting on with your friends. Only once, and that after Mary McNiven had come to take poor Myra away, did the subject of the green ray crop up.

"Mr. Burnham knows about it all, I suppose?" the General asked.

"I've told him everything, and Garnesk and I went over the whole thing with him before the train went."

"Good!" said the old man emphatically. "Excellent fellow Garnesk—excellent; in fact, I don't know when I've met such a thundering good chap. No new developments, I suppose?"

I hesitated. I could not have brought myself to lie to him, and in view of the startling complications with which we had so recently been confronted, I was at a loss for an answer. Dennis came to my rescue just in time.

"I think Ron's difficulty is in defining the word 'developments,' General," said he. "If we said there were developments it would naturally convey the impression that we had something definite to report. I think perhaps the best way to put it would be that we believe we are getting on the right scent, by the simple process of putting two and two together and making them four. We hope to have something very decided to tell you in a day or two."

"I shall be glad to hear something, I can assure you," said the old man, "but in the meantime we will try to forget about it. You have had a tiring journey, Mr. Burnham, followed by a strange initiation into what is probably a new sphere of life altogether—the sphere of mysteries and detectives, and so forth. No, Ronald, we'll give Mr. Burnham a rest for to-night."

But just as I was congratulating myself that we had escaped from the painful necessity of putting him off with an evasive answer, if not a deliberate lie, the butler entered and announced that he had shown Mr. Hilderman into the library.

"Well, as we are ready, we had better join him," said the old man, and we adjourned to the other room.

Now if Hilderman should by any tactless remark betray our strange experience in the afternoon there would be the devil to pay. I followed the General into the library, beckoning to the American with a warning finger on my lip. He saw at once what I meant, fortunately, and held his tongue, and we all talked of general matters for some little time. Then Hilderman took the bull by the horns.

"As a matter of fact, General," he announced boldly, "I ran over to have a word with Mr. Ewart about a certain matter which is interesting us all. I don't suppose you wish me to worry you with details at the moment?"

"I should be very glad to hear what you have to tell us, Mr. Hilderman, but unfortunately I—er—I have a few letters I simply must write, so I hope you will excuse me. My daughter is in the drawing-room, so perhaps you fellows would care to join her there. Her counsel will be of more use to you than mine in your deliberations, I have no doubt."

However, when we looked for her in the drawing-room Myra was not there, and I found her in her den.

"Why not bring him in here?" she asked. "He won't bite, and it will be more conducive to a free and easy discussion. I should like to hear what he has to say for himself in view of his running away this afternoon, and I shouldn't feel comfortable in the drawing-room with this shade on. In here I feel that he must just put up with any curiosities he meets."

So we made ourselves comfortable in the den, and Hilderman sat in a chair by the window.

"Of course, you know what I have come to speak about, Mr. Ewart," he began at once. "You must have thought my conduct this afternoon was very strange—very unsportsmanlike, to say the least."

"Oh, I don't know," I replied as lightly as I could. "It was a very strange affair, and it rather called for strange conduct of one sort or another."

"Still, you must have thought it cowardly to run away as quickly as I could," he insisted.

"It was some time before we even noticed you had left us," I laughed, "and then, I confess, I couldn't quite make out where you had got to or why you had gone."

"As a matter of fact we were rather scared," Dennis put in. "We searched for you in the river."

"It sounds a very cowardly confession to make," Hilderman admitted, "but I went back to the landing-stage, got into my boat, and cleared off as quickly as I could. I must ask you to believe that I was under the impression that it would be best for us all that I should. But my idea proved to be a bad one and nothing came of it. So here I am to ask you if you have learned anything or have anything to suggest."

"I'm afraid we're more at a loss than ever now," I admitted. "The further we get with this thing the less we seem to know about it, unfortunately."

Hilderman was exceedingly sympathetic, and though he made numerous suggestions he was as puzzled as we were ourselves. I had some difficulty in defining his attitude. We knew as much as was sufficient to hang his friend "Fuller," but I could not make up my mind whether he really was a friend of von Guernstein's or not. It was a small thing that decided me. On an occasionable table beside the American lay a steel paper-knife, a Japanese affair, with a carved handle and a very sharp blade. Hilderman picked up the knife and toyed with it.

"I should be careful with that, Mr. Hilderman," I advised. "That is a wolf in sheep's clothing; it's exceedingly sharp."

"Oh, yes!" cried Myra. "If you mean my paper-knife, it ought not really to be used as a paper-knife at all, the point is like a needle. I must put it away or hang it up as an ornament."

The American laughed and laid the knife down again on the table, and we resumed our discussion. Both Dennis and I knew that we must be very careful to conceal our suspicions, but at the same time we did our best to reach some sort of conclusion with regard to Hilderman himself.

"And, I suppose, until you have searched about the Saddle," he remarked, "you will be no further on as to who stole Miss McLeod's dog. It seems to me that the dog was taken by the man who wished to conceal an illicit still, and the green flash, or green ray, or whatever you call it, is simply a manifestation of some strange electrical combination in the air."

"I'm afraid we shall have to leave it at that," I said with an elaborate sigh of regret.

"Not when you have Mr. Burnham's distinguished powers of deduction to assist you, surely, Mr. Ewart?" said Hilderman, and waited for an answer.

"Flukes are not very consistent things, I fear," Dennis supplied him readily, "and if we are to make any progress we shall hardly have time for idle speculation."

"Fortune might continue to favour you," the American persisted. "Don't you think it's worth trying?"

"I'm afraid not," said Dennis, with a laugh that added emphasis and conviction to his statement.

"By the way," Myra suggested, "I don't know if anybody would care for a whisky and soda or anything. I won't have drinks served in here, but if anybody would like one, you know where everything is, Ron. I always say if anyone wants a drink in my den they can go and get it, and then I know they really like being in the den. You see I'm a woman, Mr. Hilderman," she laughed.

"I must say I think the idea of refreshment would not enter the head of anyone who had the pleasure of

your company here, Miss McLeod, unless you
suggested it yourself."

We laughed at the rather heavy compliment, and
I went into the dining-room to fetch the decanters,
syphons and glasses.

"I'll help you to get them," called Dennis, and
followed me out of the room.

"Well?" I asked as soon as we reached the other
room. "What do you make of it?"

"I'm not sure," Dennis admitted. "I'm puzzled. I
shouldn't be surprised if he turned out to be a
Government secret service man keeping an eye on
Fuller-von-Guernstein, and that when he has quite
made up his mind that the mystery of the green ray
is connected with his own business he will show his
hand."

"Something of the same sort occurred to
Garnesk," I said. "Well, at present we'd better avoid
suspicion and go back before he thinks we're holding
a committee meeting."

So I led the way to the den. I was walking
carefully and slowly, because I was unaccustomed to
carrying trays of glasses and things, and
consequently I made no noise. I pushed the door
open with my shoulder, Dennis following with a
couple of syphons, and as I did so I chanced to glance
upwards.

In a large mirror which hung over the fireplace I
saw the reflection of Hilderman's face, knitted in a
fierce frown, gazing intently at some object which
was outside my view. Myra was talking, though
what she was saying I did not notice. I went into the
room and put the tray on the big table, and as I filled
the glasses I looked round casually to see what

Hilderman had been looking at. Lying on the sofa on which Myra was sitting was the copy of the *Pictures*, open at the page bearing the incriminating photograph!

I mixed Hilderman's drink according to his instructions—for by this time he had entirely recovered his equanimity—and handed it to him. As I did so I happened to look in the direction of the small table beside him. Myra's Japanese paper-knife was still there, but the point had been stuck more than an inch into the mahogany top of the table. I turned away quickly, with a laughing remark to Myra, which did not seem to raise any suspicion at the time, though I have no recollection now what it was I said.

A few moments afterwards I quietly and unostentatiously slipped out of the room. Surely there could be no doubt about it now. The whole thing was obvious. Hilderman had noticed the paper, jumped to the conclusion that we suspected everything, and in the sudden access of baffled rage had picked up the paper-knife and stabbed it into the table.

There was only one possible reason for that— Hilderman was an enemy. In that case, I thought, he has come here to try and find out how much we know and to keep an eye on us. Possibly he might be attempting to keep us there so that Fuller could get up to some satanic trick elsewhere. I decided to act at once. I turned back to the den and put my head round the door.

"Will you people excuse me for a bit?" I said lightly. "The General wants me." And with that I left them. I had almost asked Hilderman not to go till I

came back, but I was afraid it might sound
suspicious to his acute ears. I hardly knew what to
do. I should have liked to have been able to speak
with Dennis, if only for a moment. Indeed, I am quite
ready to confess that just then I would have given all
I possessed for ten minutes' conversation with my
friend. I stole quietly out of the house, and thought
furiously.

If Hilderman wanted to keep us from spying on
Fuller, where was Fuller? Would I be wiser to wait
and try to keep an eye on Hilderman, or was my best
plan to ignore him and try and locate his German
friend? I decided on the latter course. I went back
and wrote a short note to Dennis and slipped it
inside his cap.

"I'm convinced they are both enemies. Take care
of Myra. I may be out all night. Don't let her worry
about me; I may not be back for some time, but I
shall come back all right.—R."

I left this for my friend, knowing that sooner or
later he would find it, and went down to the landing-
stage. The *Baltimore II.* and Myra's boat, the *Jenny
Spinner*, were drawn up alongside, and I realised
that if I took the *Jenny* I should be raising
Hilderman's suspicions at once. Anchored a little
way out was another small motor-boat—the first the
General had—which Myra had also called after a
trout fly—the *Coch-a-Bondhu*—though the play
upon words was lost on most people. The boat was
still in constant use, and Angus and Hamish
continually went into Mallaig and Glenelg in it to
collect parcels and so on. I ran to the petrol shed,
and got three tins of Shell, put them in the dinghy
and pushed out to the *Bondhu*, climbed on board,

sounded the tank, filled it up, and started out across the Loch. I can only plead my anxiety to get well out of sight and hearing before Hilderman should think of leaving the house, as an excuse for my lamentable thoughtlessness on this occasion. Indeed, it was not till long afterwards that I realised I had forgotten to anchor the dinghy, and I left it, just as it was, to drift out to sea on the tide.

I made all the pace I could and reached the other side in about twenty minutes. I was sadly equipped for an adventurous expedition! I had no flask to sustain me in case of need, no weapon in case I should be called to defend myself; I was wearing a dinner-jacket, no hat, and a pair of thin patent-leather pumps!

I ran the boat right in shore, heedless of the danger to the propeller, in a small sandy cove round the point, so that I was hidden from Glasnabinnie. Then I realised that I had been a little too precipitate in my departure. There was no anchor-chain on board, and the painter was admirably suited for making fast to pier-heads and landing-stages at high tide, but was nothing like long enough to enable me to make the craft secure on short. However, I dragged her as far up as I could, and prayed that I might be able to return before the tide caught her up and carried her away. In those circumstances I should have been stranded in the enemy's country, by no means a pleasing prospect!

Having done the best I could for Myra's faithful motor-boat, I made my way round the hill, climbing cautiously upwards all the time, my dinner-jacket carefully buttoned in case a gleam of moonlight on my shirt-front should give me away at a critical moment. It was a rocky and difficult climb, and I soon regretted that I had not taken the bridle path to Glasnabinnie and made my way boldly up the bed of the burn. However, it was too late to turn back, and eventually, after one or two false steps and stumbles, I succeeded in reaching a spot from which I could obtain a good view of the hut. No, there was no light there, no sign of movement at all. I decided to work my way round to the other side and then, if I continued to get no satisfaction, to descend to the house. The windows of the hut, or smoking-room, as the reader will no doubt remember, extended the whole length of the structure; and surely, I thought, if there were a light in the place it would be bound to be visible. I edged round the face of a steep crag, floundered across the stream between the two falls, getting myself soaked above the knees as I did so, and crouched among the heather on the other side of the building. No, there was no one there, the place was deserted. I knelt down and peered about me listening intently.

Not a sound greeted my expectant ear save the incessant rumble of the falls. Then as I turned my attention to the house itself and looked down the course of the burn to Glasnabinnie, I could scarcely suppress a cry of astonishment. For there below me, moving to and fro between the house and the hut, was a constant procession of small lights, like a slowly moving stream of glow-worms, twenty or thirty yards apart. I was rooted to the spot. What could it mean? Was this another weird natural manifestation, or was it, as was much more likely, a couple of dozen men bearing lights? Yes, that was it, men bearing lights—and what else besides? Men don't climb up and down steep watercourses in the night for the sake of giving an impromptu firework display to an unexpected visitor, I told myself. There was only one thing to do, and that was to investigate the matter and chance what might happen to me. I crept down to the hut, and lay on my face among the heather and listened. Here and there a mumble of voices, now and then a subdued shout, apparently an order to be carried out by the mysterious light-bearers, broken occasionally by the shrill call of a gull, conveyed nothing to me that I could not see. I looked up at the hut. No, there was no one there, and the windows were not screened, because I could see the moonlight streaming through the far side. Yet, surely, the hut must be their objective, I thought. Where else could they be going to? Fascinated, I crawled on my hands and knees till I could touch the walls of the smoking-room by putting out my arm. I heard a great commotion coming, it seemed, from the very ground beneath my feet.

I laid my ear to the ground and listened. The noise grew louder, and the voices seemed to be shouting against a more powerful sound—the waterfall, possibly. I thought perhaps the floor of the hut would give me more opportunity to locate the source of the disturbance. I threw caution to the winds and slipped through the wide windows into the room. I moved as carefully as I could, however, once my feet found the floor, for if there should be anyone below they would probably hear me up above. I turned back the carpet in order to hear more distinctly, and as I did so I noticed a rectangular shaft of light which trickled through the floor. There was a trap-door. I knelt down and lifted it cautiously by a leather tab which was attached to one side of it and peered through. I can never understand how it was I did not drop that hatch again with a self-confessing crash when I realised the extraordinary nature of the sight that greeted my eyes. There was I in the smoking-hut of a peaceful American citizen, where only a few hours before I had spent a pleasant hour in friendly conversation, and now I was lying on the edge of the entrance to a great cavern.

Below me there was a confused mass of machinery and men. Some were working on scaffolding, others were many feet below. The nearest of them was so close to me that I could have leaned down and laid my hand on his head. I tried to make out what they were doing, but except that they were dismantling the machinery, whatever it might be, I could make nothing of it. I watched them breathlessly, trembling lest at any moment one of them should look up and detect my presence.

The place was lighted by electricity, though there were not enough lamps to illuminate the cavern very brightly, and as my eyes got accustomed to the lights and shadows I was able to make out the cause of this.

Evidently there was a turbine engine below, driven by the water from the falls, which supplied the necessary power. After a moment or two it dawned on me how the cavern came to be there; it was, or had been, the course of a hidden river, such as are common enough among the mountains, but the stream had been diverted, probably by some sort of landslide, and had left this tumbler-shaped cave, resembling a pit shaft. Now, I thought, I have only to find out what all this machinery is for and the whole mystery is solved. I opened the trap a little further, and allowed my body to hang slightly over the edge.

Then for the first time I saw, to my right, fixed so that it almost touched the floor of the hut, a great round brass object, mounted on an enormous tripod, which, again, stood on a platform. In front of this was a large square thing like a mammoth rectangular condenser, such as is used for photographic enlarging and other projection purposes. Had it not been for this condenser I should have taken the whole thing to be an elaborate searchlight. But, I asked myself, what would be the good of a searchlight there? Suddenly the whole truth dawned upon me.

The searchlight must operate through a trap in the wall of the hut just below the floor. I leaned further in, forgetting my danger in the intoxication of sudden discovery.

Only a foot or two away from me a man was working on the searchlight. Carefully taking it to pieces, he was handing the parts to another man, who was perched on the scaffold below him. He was so close to me that I could hear him breathing. I was about to wriggle back to safety when he looked up. He gave a sudden loud shout. I lay there fascinated. After all, I thought, before they can reach me I can slip out and edge round the cliff, run down on to the shore, and get away in the motor-boat. But I had reckoned without my host. Even as the man shouted, and the others left their work to see what was the matter, Fuller dashed out from behind the platform, gave one terrified look at me, and, flinging himself at the wall of the cavern, threw all his weight on a rope which dangled there. I scuttled to my feet, intending to make a bolt for it. But the boards shivered beneath me, and, before I could realise what was happening, I found myself hurtling through the air to the floor of the cavern below.

Chapter XVII. Some Grave Fears

And now, as the reader will readily understand, I must continue the story as it was afterwards related to me.

Myra, the General, and Dennis sat up and waited for me till the early hours of the morning, but I did not return. The young people did what they could to assure the old man that my sudden and unexpected disappearance had been entirely voluntary, and Dennis, who had found my note, as soon as he put on his cap to stroll out casually, and see where I had got to, gave him subtly to understand that it was really part of a prearranged plan, and Myra at length persuaded him to go to bed at midnight.

When I failed to put in an appearance at breakfast-time, however, even they began to be a trifle alarmed, but they did their best to conceal their fears. They scoured the hillside and then went down to the landing-stage. Dennis had reported the previous night that the motor-boat was still in its place when he saw Hilderman off, and it never occurred to Myra that I might make my departure in the *Coch-a-Bondhu.*

"He hasn't gone by the sea, any way," Dennis announced again, as he and the girl stood on the landing-stage.

"You mean the *Jenny* is still there?" she asked.

"Yes," said Dennis, "she's just where she was when we arrived from Glasnabinnie in Hilderman's boat yesterday."

"Mr. Burnham!" Myra cried suddenly, "is there another boat, a brown motor-boat, anchored just out there?"

"No," said Dennis, realising how terribly handicapped they were by Myra's inability to see.

"Are you sure?" the girl asked anxiously.

"Quite sure," said Dennis positively. "There is one motor-boat here, and that is all."

"I suppose he took that to put Hilderman off the scent," Myra mused, "and in that case he is probably quite safe. I daresay he's gone to look for our friend von What's-his name's yacht or his house at Loch Duich."

Dennis clutched at the opportunity this theory gave him to allay her fears, and declared that it was ridiculous of him not to have thought of it before, and he gave Myra his arm to the house. But he was not at all satisfied with it, and, as it turned out afterwards, Myra was not very confident about it either. Dennis knew me well enough to know that I should never have set out with the deliberate intention of stopping away overnight without leaving some more definite message for my *fiancee*. However, their thoughts were speedily diverted, for they had hardly reached the house before a strange man made his way towards them through the heather.

"Mr. Ewart, sir?" he asked.

"Do you wish to speak to Mr. Ewart?" Dennis asked cautiously.

"I have a parcel and a message for him from Mr. Garnesk," said the stranger, a young man, who might have been anything by profession.

"Oh, indeed," said Dennis, his suspicions aroused at once. Garnesk, he knew, had only arrived in Glasgow the night before.

"I see you are wondering how I got here and why I came down the hill, instead of up a road of some sort," said the youth with a smile.

"Frankly, I was," Dennis admitted.

"Then, perhaps, I had better explain who I am and how I come to be here. My name is McKenzie. I am employed by Welton and Delaunay, the Glasgow opticians, makers of the 'Weldel' telescopes and binoculars. Mr. Garnesk has a good deal to do with our firm in the matter of designs for special glasses to withstand furnace heat, for ironworkers, etc. He arrived at the works last night in a car, and, after consulting with the manager, they kept a lot of us at work all night on a new design of spectacles.

"I was sent with this parcel in the early hours of the morning. There was no passenger train, but Mr. Garnesk got me a military pass on a fish train, and here I am. I was to deliver the parcel to Mr. Ewart, or, failing him, to Miss McLeod. When I saw this lady with the—er—the shade over her eyes I thought you were probably Mr. Ewart, sir."

"I'm not, as a matter of fact," said Dennis. "But where have you come from, and why didn't you come up the path?"

"Mr. Garnesk gave me instructions, sir, which I read to the boatman who brought me here. Mr. Garnesk said I would find several fishermen at Mallaig who had motor-boats, and would bring me across. He also gave me this paper, and told me on no account to deviate from the directions he gave."

Dennis held out his hand for the paper. He glanced through it, and then read it to Myra.

"Take a motor-boat from Mallaig to Invermalluch Lodge," he read. "Tell the man to cross the top of Loch Hourn as if he were going to Glenelg, but when he gets well round the point he is to double back, and land you as near as he can to the house, but to keep on the far side of the point. You are on no account to be taken to the landing-stage at the lodge. When you arrive at the lodge insist on seeing Mr. Ewart, or Miss McLeod personally, if Mr. Ewart is not there. Then rejoin your motor-boat, and go on to Glenelg. Wait there for the first boat that will take you to Mallaig, and come back by the train. Do not return to Mallaig by motor-boat."

"Those are very elaborate instructions, Mr. Burnham," said Myra. "It would seem that Mr. Garnesk is very suspicious about something."

"Evidently," Dennis agreed. "You'd better let Miss McLeod have that parcel," he added to McKenzie. The youth handed him the parcel, and at Myra's suggestion Dennis opened it. Topmost among its contents was a letter addressed to me. Dennis tore it open and read it.

"Miss McLeod is to wear a pair of these glasses until I see her again. She will be able to see through them fairly well, but she must not remove them. The consequences might be fatal. The three other pairs are for you and Burnham, and one extra in case of accidents. It will also come in handy if you take Hilderman into your confidence. Wear these glasses when you are in any danger of coming in contact with the green ray. I have an idea that they will act as a decided protection. I also enclose one Colt automatic pistol and cartridges, the only one I could get in the middle of the night. If you decide to ask Hilderman's help tell him everything. I am sure he will be very useful to you. Keep your courage up, old man! The best to you all. In haste.—H.G."

"We're certainly learning something," said Dennis, as he finished. "Obviously Garnesk is very suspicious of somebody, but it's not Hilderman. He writes as if he were pretty sure of himself. Probably he has proved his theory about Hilderman being a Government detective."

"I have a message for Mr. Ewart, sir," the messenger interrupted.

"You had better tell it me," Dennis suggested.

"I'd rather Miss McLeod asked me," McKenzie demurred. "Those were Mr. Garnesk's instructions. He said 'failing Mr. Ewart, insist on seeing Miss McLeod.'"

"Very well," laughed Myra. "I quite appreciate your point. May I know the message?"

"Mr. Ewart was to take no notice whatever of anything Mr. Garnesk said in his letter about Mr. Hilderman. He was on no account to trust Mr. Hilderman, but to be very careful not to let him see he was suspected. The gentlemen were always to wear their glasses whenever they were in sight of the hut above—Glas.—above Mr. Hilderman's house."

"Whew!" Dennis whistled. "But why didn't he—— ? Oh, I see. He was afraid the letter might fall into Hilderman's hands."

"I wonder where Ron can have got to?" Myra mused wistfully.

"We're very much obliged to you for all the trouble you have taken, Mr. McKenzie," said Dennis. "You've done very well indeed."

"Oh, Mr. Garnesk also said that Miss McLeod was to put on her glasses by the red light."

"Yes; that's important," Dennis agreed. "We'll go up to the house now, shall we, Miss McLeod?"

"Yes," said Myra, "and Mr. McKenzie must come and have a meal and a rest, as I'm sure he needs both after his journey. I'll send Angus to look after the boatman." So the three strolled up to the lodge.

"By the way," said Dennis, "of course it's all right, and you've carried out your instructions to the letter, but how can you be sure this is Miss McLeod, and how do you know I'm not Hilderman?"

"Mr. Garnesk described everybody I should be likely to meet," McKenzie replied, "including Mr. Hilderman and Mr. Fuller. I know you are Mr. Ewart's friend because you have a small white scar above your left eyebrow. So, being with you, and wearing a shade and an Indian bangle, I thought I was safe in concluding the lady was Miss McLeod."

"Garnesk doesn't seem to miss much!" Dennis laughed.

"He made me repeat his descriptions about twenty times," said McKenzie, "so I felt pretty sure of myself."

When they got up to the lodge, and the messenger's requirements had been administered to, Dennis unpacked the parcel. The spectacles proved to be something like motor goggles; they fitted closely over the nose and forehead, and entirely excluded all light except that which could be seen through the glass. The only curious thing about them was the glass itself. Instead of being white, or even blue, it was red, and the surface was scratched diagonally in minute parallel lines. Myra and Dennis hurried upstairs, and lighted the lamp in the darkroom. When the girl came down again she declared that she could see beautifully. Everything was red, of course, but she could see quite distinctly.

"Have you any idea why these glasses are ruled in lines like this?" Dennis asked McKenzie.

"I couldn't say for certain, sir," the youth replied. "But I should think it was because Mr. Garnesk thought the glasses would be so near the eye as to be ineffective. In photography, for instance, you can't print either bromide or printing-out paper in a red light. But if you coat a red glass with emulsion, and make an exposure on it, you can print the negative in the usual way. I don't know why it is."

"Perhaps there is no space for a ray to form," Myra suggested.

"You must tell Mr. Garnesk how deeply grateful we all are to him," said Dennis. "I'll give you a letter to take back to him. It has been a wonderfully quick bit of work!"

"I should think he has got some hundreds of the glasses finished by this time," said McKenzie, "and he has already asked for an estimate for fifty thousand of them."

"Whatever for?" Myra exclaimed.

"I couldn't say at all, but Mr. Garnesk probably has it all mapped out. He always knows what he's about."

A couple of hours later McKenzie left for Glenelg, with ample time to catch his boat, and the others sat down to lunch. Myra was delighted that she could

see, even though everything was red. Just as they
had finished lunch a telegram was delivered to
Dennis. It was handed in at Mallaig, and it read:
"Don't worry about me. May be away for a few
days.—EWART."

"Oh, good!" exclaimed Dennis. "A wire from Ron.
He's all right. 'Don't worry about me. May be away
for a few days.' Sent from Mallaig. He may have got
something he feels he must tell Garnesk about, and
has gone to Glasgow."

"I expect that's it," Myra agreed. "I'm glad he's
wired. I do hope he'll write from wherever he is to-
night. Do you think I shall get a letter in the
morning?"

"Certain to," Dennis vowed, laying the telegram
on the mantelpiece. "He's sure to write, however
busy he is."

Though Myra was disappointed that there was no
personal message for her, she tried to believe that
everything was all right. Dennis went on what he
called coastguard duty, and watched the sea and
shores with the untiring loyalty of a faithful dog.
That night, after dinner, he went out to keep an eye
on things, and left Myra with her father. She has
told me since that she felt miserable that I had not
wired to her, and went to fetch my telegram in order
to get what comfort she could from my message to
Dennis. She held the telegram under the light, and
read it through. The words were: "May be away for a
few days.—EWART." She made out the faint pencil
writing slowly through the red glass. She read it
twice through, and then suddenly collapsed into an
armchair in the horror of swift realisation. "Ewart!"
she whispered, "Ewart! He would never sign a

telegram to Mr. Burnham in that way. If Ronnie didn't send that wire, who did?"

In a moment she jumped to her feet. She must act, and act quickly.

She ran into the den, and picked up the revolver and cartridges which Garnesk had sent, and which she had put carefully away until I should come and claim them. She loaded the revolver, and tucked it in the pocket of the Burberry coat which she slipped on in the hall. Then she tore down to the landing-stage, and made straight for Glasnabinnie in the *Jenny Spinner*. She had got about half a mile when Dennis, coming up to the top of the cliff on his self-imposed coastguard duties, saw her and recognised her through his binoculars.

He ran down to the landing-stage, putting on his red glasses as he went. His horror was complete when he found there was no craft of any kind about, not even a rowboat. Alas! I had idiotically allowed the dinghy to drift away. He ran along the shore, every now and then looking anxiously through his binoculars for any sign of any kind of boat that would get him over to Glasnabinnie in time to fulfil his promise of looking after "Ron's little girl."

Myra has since admitted—and how proud I was to hear her say it—that she forgot about everything and everybody except that I was in danger, and probably Hilderman knew something about it. Her one thought was to hold the pistol to his head and demand my safe return.

She came ashore a little beyond the house, having made a rather wide detour, so that she should not be seen. She knew the best way to the hut, and there was a light in it. She thought

Hilderman would be there. She had passed well to seaward of the *Fiona*, and noticed that she was standing by with steam up. Myra climbed the hill to the hut with as much speed as she could.

Hilderman was standing below the door of the smoking-room talking to three men. She knew that she would have no chance, even with a revolver, against four men. She might hurt one of them, but she recognised, fortunately, that the others would overpower her.

Eventually Hilderman went into the hut, and two of the men stayed outside talking. The other went down the hill. It was in watching this man that Myra saw the sight that had astonished me, the continuous stream of lights down the bed of the burn. She waited, so she said it seemed, for hours and hours, before she could see a real chance of attacking Hilderman.

Indeed, neither she nor Dennis can give any very clear idea precisely how long it was that she waited there, but it must have been a considerable time. At last Hilderman was alone. Myra crept to the edge of the little plateau on which the hut stood, and then made a dash for the door. She thrust it open and stepped inside, pulling it to behind her. Hilderman sprang to his feet with an oath as he saw her.

"Heavens!" he cried. "You!"

Myra drew the revolver and presented it at him.

"Put up your hands, Mr. Hilderman," she said, with a calmness that astonished herself, "and tell me what you have done with Ronnie—Mr. Ewart."

"I must admit you've caught me, Miss McLeod!" Hilderman replied. "I can only assure you that your *fiance* is safe."

"Where is he?" Myra asked.

"He is quite close at hand," Hilderman assured her, "and quite safe. What do you want me to do?"

"You must set him free at once," said Myra quietly.

"And if I refuse?"

"I shall shoot you and anyone else who comes near me."

"Now look here, Miss McLeod," said Hilderman, "I may be prepared to come to terms with you. If you shot me and half a dozen others it would not help you to find Mr. Ewart. On the other hand, it would be awkward for us to have a lot of shooting going on, and I have no wish to harm Mr. Ewart. If I produce him, and allow you two to go away, are you prepared to swear to me that you will neither of you breathe a word of anything you may know to any living soul for forty-eight hours? I think I can trust you."

Myra thought it over quickly.

"Yes," she said, "if you will——"

But she never finished the sentence. At that moment someone caught her wrist in a grip of steel, and wrenched the pistol from her.

"Come, come, Miss McLeod," said Fuller. "This is very un-neighbourly of you."

Myra looked round her in despair. There must be some way out of this. She cudgelled her brains to devise some means of getting the better of her captives. Fuller laid the pistol on the table and sat down.

"You need not be alarmed," he said. "We shall not hurt you. You will be left here, that is all. And we shall get safely away. After this we shall not be able to leave your precious lover with you, but Hilderman insists that he shall not be hurt, and we shall take him to Germany and treat him as a prisoner of war."

Then Myra had an inspiration. She turned her head towards Fuller, as if she were looking about two feet to the right of his head.

"You may as well kill me as leave me here," she said calmly.

"Nonsense," said Hilderman. "If we leave you here, and see that you have no means of getting away by sea, you will have to find your way across the hills or round the cliffs. There is no road, and by the time you return to civilisation we shall be clear."

"That's very thoughtful of you," said Myra. "You bargain on my falling over a precipice or something. A blind girl would have a splendid chance of getting back safely!"

"Good heavens!" Hilderman cried. "I thought you must be able to see. Fuller, this means that that fellow Burnham came with her, and is close at hand. What in the name——"

But he, too, was interrupted, for a great, gaunt figure flashed like some weird animal through the window. A long bare arm reached over Fuller's shoulder and snatched the pistol.

"Yes, Mr. Burnham is with her," said Dennis quietly, as he stood in front of them, stripped to the waist, the water pouring off him in streams, and covered them with the revolver.

Hilderman and Fuller von Guernstein held up their hands as requested.

"This is very awkward," said Fuller. "We shall have to let that wretched Ewart go."

And then Dennis swayed, threw up his arms, and fell sideways, full length on the floor. Myra glanced at him, and threw herself on her knees beside the prostrate form.

"Dead!" she screamed. "*Dead!*"

Hilderman pushed her gently aside, and knelt down to examine Dennis.

"It's his heart," he announced. "Come Hugo. We're safe now, and the girl's blind. Let's get away."

CHAPTER XVIII. THE TRUTH REVEALED

I will here resume my own narrative.

When I came to myself I was dazed and aching, but, so far as I could discover, there were no bones broken. The curious part about it was the rapidity with which I recalled my fall into the cavern. When I found I could move my limbs freely I sat up, and discovered that I was in a small cabin on board a steamer. I stood up and stretched myself. I was feeling weak and ill, but that would pass off I thought. A minute's speculation decided me that I was on board the *Fiona*, in which case I was shanghaied.

I knew that if I valued my life I must act at once. I opened the door of the cabin, and was surprised to find that it was unlocked. Then I crept cautiously in the shadows of the dawn up the companion-ladder to the deck. Though I heard voices I could see no one close to me. I stole along the deck and listened. The voices were talking quite freely in German. Where could we be? And, more important still, where were we going?

I looked around me, and saw that we were steaming slowly down a narrow loch, surrounded by mountains which stretched right down to the shores. I looked across the deck and almost shouted out in my surprise. For there, moving gracefully alongside of us, was a submarine. There were two officers on the deck of the submarine chatting with Hilderman and Fuller, who were leaning over the rail of the

Fiona. A submarine! A German submarine in a peaceful Scottish loch! Then this was the secret base we had discussed. I looked up at the wheel-house. In front of it was the very searchlight, with its curious condenser that I had seen in the cavern.

What could it mean? I decided to slip overboard unseen, if possible, swim to the shore, and get back over the rocks to the mouth of the loch, and give the alarm if I should be fortunate enough to attract the attention of any passing steamer.

But suddenly an idea struck me. I crept quickly up the ladder to the deckhouse, threw my arms round the man at the wheel, flung him down on to the deck, and swung the wheel round with all the strength I had in me. There was a dull, crunching sound as the yacht lurched round. A groaning shiver shook her, and, if I may be pardoned the illustration, it felt exactly as if the ship were going to be sick. There were hoarse cries from the men, and as the *Fiona* righted herself I looked astern. There was a frothy, many-coloured effervescence of oil and water.

The submarine had disappeared! The yacht was nearing the head of the loch. It was now or never. I made a dash for the side, but Fuller was before me. He tripped me up, and I fell heavily to the deck, bruising myself badly and giving my head a terrible bump. I put up my arm in a last feeble attempt to defend myself. Fuller's hands closed on my throat and nearly choked the life out of me, and as I sank back, struggling for breath, a loud cry rang out from Hilderman.

"Guernstein! Guernstein!" he yelled.

Fuller let me go and ran to Hilderman. I lifted myself on my elbow. Somehow or other I would crawl to the side, and get away before he came back to finish me, but as I looked out over the stern I was rooted to the spot by the sight that met my eyes. Or was I deluding myself with the fantastic delirium of a dying man? Not four hundred yards away was a motor-boat. It was Hilderman's *Baltimore II.*, and in it were Myra, my poor Myra, and Garnesk and Angus, all wearing motor-goggles. But, strangest of all, a British destroyer was puffing serenely behind them. No, I must be dreaming. Garnesk had told me he was sending glasses for Myra. He had mentioned his connection with the naval authorities. This must be the nightmare of death-agony.

Then Fuller rushed up the wheel-house ladder and jumped on to the searchlight platform. Suddenly there flashed out on the grey light of the dawn a vivid green ray. So, then, the mystery was solved— but, alas! too late. The green ray was produced by a searchlight, and every man on the destroyer would be blind. I looked back, and as I did so I remembered, with an uncanny distinctness, old General McLeod's words, "The rock came to me." The warship seemed suddenly to grow double its size, and then double that, and so on, growing bigger and bigger until it appeared to fill the entire loch, and spread out the whole length of the horizon. I could even see a gold signet-ring on the finger of a young officer on the bridge. I looked round at the details of the boat; it stood out in amazing clearness. If one man on that ship, hundreds of yards away, had opened his mouth I could have counted his teeth. Suddenly I gasped with astonishment as I awoke to the fact that every man on board the destroyer was wearing motor-goggles! I had no time to speculate about this new surprise, for then the *Fiona*, left to her own devices, suddenly crashed ashore. The ship shook and shivered, and Fuller was thrown on his face beside the searchlight, and as I looked again the destroyer had resumed its normal proportions.

Then the crew of the *Fiona* rushed about the deck in mad terror, until, evidently at the wise suggestion of one of their number, they decided to wait calmly and give themselves up. Hilderman, closely followed by Fuller, sprang ashore, and made for the mountains. Half a dozen shots rang out from the destroyer, and a rifle bullet checked Fuller's progress before he had gone more than a few yards.

Hilderman, however, managed to reach the shelter of a ridge of rock, and I watched him as he scuttled up the mountain side, and made straight for a long grey rock which protruded from the foot of a steep crag. And as I looked, and saw him go to the rock and open a door in it, I realised that it was really a great, grey, lean-to shed, cunningly concealed. Hilderman had scarcely opened the door when a huge, dark shadow seemed to fall out of the shed and envelop him. It was Sholto. Blind, and half-mad with fury, he sprang at Hilderman's throat with the unerring aim of his breed. The wretched man staggered and fell, and Sholto——.

I turned away from the sickening sight, and looked over the side, and saw Myra standing up, waving to me, as they drew alongside the wrecked *Fiona*.

And then I'm afraid I must have fainted.

*   *   *   *   *

I lay on the sofa in Myra's den, and Myra—God bless her!—was kneeling beside me. Sholto was with us too, looking incredibly wise in a pair of motor-goggles.

"So you see, darling," said Myra, "the glasses cured me completely, and I can see just as well as ever." And I shall not repeat what I said in reply to such glorious news.

"Tell me, dear," I asked shortly, "what exactly happened with Dennis? I haven't quite got that."

"Well, he saw me on my way to Glasnabinnie," she explained, "and was determined to follow. He couldn't find a boat of any kind, so he swam! Angus saw him in the water and ran and told daddy. When they found there was no boat they went and fetched the one on the loch, carried it down to the sea, and called Hamish. Then they pulled across. Then, you see, when Dennis had his heart attack, I thought he was only pretending. I thought he saw that we should never be able to get away again, and that if he pretended to be dead they would leave us alone. So I followed his lead. I was terribly frightened when I couldn't make him answer me after they had gone, but before I could do anything daddy and the men arrived. Angus stopped with me, and told me where the *Fiona* had gone. We took the *Baltimore* because she is much faster than our boat. He must have been a duffer to lose that race we had. And then daddy and Hamish took Dennis—I refuse to call him Mr. Burnham after this—and brought him here and sent for Dr. Whitehouse."

"I'm thankful he's out of danger," I said fervently.

"But the doctor says he must take it very, very gently for a long time, and he won't be able to walk

much for months. Did he know he had this heart
trouble?"

I had scarcely finished explaining the extent of
Dennis's heroism when Garnesk arrived.

"Hilderman's dead!" he said. "He made a full
confession. It seems he is a German, and his name's
von Hilder. He has lived most of his life in America.
He is a brilliant physicist, and has done some big
things with electricity and light. He was here to
prepare the submarine base you found, and he also
got on with a new invention—The Green Ray. Of
course he didn't give the secret of that away, but we
have the searchlight, and I have already tumbled to
it partly. It is practically a new form of light.

"It is formed by passing violet and orange rays
through tourmaline and quartz respectively. The
accident to Miss McLeod was their first intimation of
its blinding properties, and to the end he knew
nothing about the suffocation part of it. I find by
experiment that when the two rays are switched on
simultaneously the air does not become de-
oxygenised, but when you put the violet ray first it
does, and it remains so until the orange ray is
applied. The effect that Hilderman imagined, and
succeeded in producing, was a ray of light which
should so alter the relative density of the air as to
act as a telescope. He's done it, and it's one of the
finest achievements of science. However, I have a
piece of wonderful news for you."

"What is it?" we both demanded at once.

"The Secret of the Green Ray is ours, and ours
alone. Hilderman has admitted that the reason why
they did not clear it out at the first sign of suspicion
was that, in their final calculations, they were

unsure of their figures. That means, put popularly, that though he knew what he was trying to do, and how he meant to do it, the actual result was something of a fluke. It very often is with inventors. They had no drawings that they could rely on to make another searchlight by, so they were bound to take the whole thing back with them. They could send no figures, because the relative distances and other quantities baffled them. They could not take the searchlight back in pieces, because if any piece had been broken they might not have been able to reconstruct the proportions with critical accuracy, as we say. So what was to have been Germany's hideous weapon of war is now ours. We have a searchlight which acts as a telescope, which will pierce the deepest fog, and which will dispel the most ungodly poisonous gases ever invented. You can see for yourself that no gas could make headway against the atmosphere you encountered the other day. Armies and navies will be absolutely powerless to advance against it. The green ray is the fourth arm of military power. So you see what you've done for your country, you lucky dog!"

"*I!*" I cried. "I like that! I've had less to do with it than anyone. What about you, eh?—coming running up with a gunboat at the critical moment. How did you manage that?"

"Well," he replied, "as soon as I was in the train on my way back I solved the problem of the fateful hour—with your help, of course. You pointed out that only then was the whole of the gorge flooded with sunshine. Now, it struck me that, if it were not electricity, it would be heat or some other form of light. Then it flashed into my mind that if it were done from a searchlight possessed of some devilish properties the light would not be visible, but the properties would continue to act. *Voila!* Then I had already—also with your help—had some doubt of von Hilder; and the hut was *the* place from which a searchlight would operate on the river. As soon as I got out of the train I taxied to my naval chief, under whom I am working throughout the war, and simply paralysed him with the whole yarn. I pitched him such a tale that he got through to the gunboat to stand by at Mallaig. They were at Portree, nice and handy. I rushed and got the glasses done for the men, picked up the destroyer at Mallaig, and made round here to find out what was happening. Then we sighted Miss McLeod and Angus, and you know the rest. Miss McLeod refused to take the shelter the warship offered, and Angus refused to leave her, so I stayed with them. We acted as pilot-boat, and there you are. That's the lot! Are you satisfied?"

"I'm satisfied, old man," I said, holding out my hand. "Some day I'll try and tell you *how* satisfied."

"Oh, that's all right," he laughed, and left us in great spirits to return to the searchlight.

And so I was left alone with Myra, who a month ago became my wife. For my services rendered in connection with the remarkable affair I received an appointment in the Naval Intelligence Department, while many of our recent successes on land and on sea have, though the truth has been withheld from the public, been due to the employment of The Green Ray.

THE END

RESURRECTED PRESS MYSTERIES FROM LOUIS TRACY

The Albert Gate Mystery
Four men murdered and a fortune in diamonds belonging to the Turkish Sultan stolen, while the Foreign Office official in charge has gone missing. Was it a common jewelry theft or was it a case of international intrigue? This is the question that barrister detective Reginald Brett must solve.

The Bartlett Mystery
When Ronald Tower is murdered on his way to a bridge game on the yacht Sans Souci it at first appears a common crime. But as Rex Carshaw finds, a tragic case of mistaken identity leads to political scandal among the rich and powerful of New York.

The Strange Case of Mortimer Fenley
When the wealthy Mortimer Fenley is struck down by a shot from an express rifle on the steps of his mansion, detectives Winter and Furneaux of Scotland Yard must find the culprit. Was it the artist who claimed he was painting a picture at the time of the shot? The disaffected younger son? Or is there another suspect?

The Stowmarket Mystery
For five generations the Fergus-Hume family has been cursed. Each of the baronets has met a violent end. When the fifth baronet is found slain by a ceremonial Japanese dagger, suspicion falls on his cousin David. It falls to barrister detective Reginald Brett to prove his innocence and find the real murder in a case that spans two continents and as many centuries.

Visit www.resurrectedpress.com

Resurrected Press Mysteries From J. S. Fletcher

The Orange-Yellow Diamond
When an elderly pawnbroker is murdered in the London parish of Paddington, a young, down on his luck writer is accused of the crime. But then it's found the pawnbroker had had in his possession an extraordinary South African diamond worth over eighty-thousand pounds — a diamond that's now missing. It falls to Melky Rubenstein to unravel the mystery and prove the young man's innocence.

The Middle Temple Murder
When an elderly man's body is found on the steps of chambers in the Midde Temple, one of the Inns of Court, it falls to newspaperman Frank Spargo and Detective-Sergeant Rathbury to solve the crime. The murdered man, for indeed it was murder, was found with no money or identification on his person except for a piece of paper with the name and address of a young barrister. Who is the victim? Why was he killed? Who is the murderer?

Scarhaven Keep
Bassett Oliver, the famed actor, has gone missing. When Oliver fails to show for a rehearsal, aspiring playwright Richard Copplestone finds himself sent to the small village of Scarhaven on the northern coast of England to track down the actors movements. What he finds is mystery. Find the answers as Copplestone unravels the mystery of Scarhaven Keep.

Visit **www.resurrectedpress.com**

RESURRECTED PRESS MYSTERIES FROM FERGUS HUME

The Green Mummy

Professor Braddock hoped to compare the burial practices of the Egyptians with those of the ancient Peruvians with his latest acquisition, the mummy of the last Inca, Caxas. But on arrival, the packing case proved to hold not the mummy, but the body of his assistant Sidney Bolton. It falls to Archie Hope to discover the murderer if he is to marry the professors step-daughter, Lucy Kendal. Who killed Bolton and where is the mummy? Was it the sea captain Hervey? The mysterious Don Pedro? Cockatoo the Polynesian servant? The professor, himself? And what has become of the emeralds? These are the questions that Hope must answer amongst the secrets of the past in The Green Mummy.

The Mystery of a Hansom Cab

"Truth is said to be stranger than fiction, and certainly the extraordinary murder which took place in Melbourne Friday morning goes a long way towards verifying that saying." Thus opens The Mystery of a Hansom Cab, the best selling mystery of the nineteenth century. When a man is found dead in a hansom cab one of Melbourne's leading citizens is accused of the murder. He pleads his innocence, yet refuses to give an alibi. It falls to a determined lawyer and an intrepid detective to find the truth, revealing long kept secrets along the way. Fergus Hume's first and perhaps most famous mystery... The Mystery Of A Hansom Cab.

Visit www.resurrectedpress.com

RESURRECTED PRESS MYSTERIES FROM THE DR. JOHN THORNDYKE SERIES

Dr. John Thorndyke - Lecturer on Medical Jurisprudence and Forensic Medicine. Before Bones, before CSI, before Quincy, M.E– there was Dr. John Thorndyke solving the most baffling cases of Edwardian London using the latest tools of medical science. Read about his cases in:

The Eye of Osiris
John Bellingham, noted Egyptologist has vanished not once but twice in the same day. Now Dr, Thorndyke must unravel the tangled claims on his estate, solve the riddle of the missing man and find the "Eye of Osiris".

The Mystery of 31 New Inn
When Dr. Jervis is whisked away in a coach with no windows to an unknown location to treat a man in a coma from undivulged causes it is Dr. Thorndyke who must come up with the solution.

The Red Thumb Mark
The first of Dr. Thorndyke's cases finds him trying to prove the innocence of a young man accused of being a diamond thief despite the fact that his finger print was found at the scene of the crime.

John Thorndyke's Cases
More cases of medical mysteries as told by his trusted assistant Jervis, M.D. Eight stories of crime and deduction in Edwardian London.

Visit www.resurrectedpress.com

Resurrected Press Mysteries by John R. Watson & Arthur J. Rees

The Hampstead Mystery
High Court Justice Sir Horace Fewbanks found shot dead in his Hampstead home, a butler with a criminal past, a scorned lover and a hint of scandal. These are the elements of the Hampstead Mystery that Detective Inspector Chippenfield of Scotland Yard must unravel with the assistance of the ambitious Detective Rolfe. But will he be able to sort out the tangled threads of this case and arrest the culprit before he is upstaged by the celebrated gentleman detective Crewe. Follow the details of this amazing case at it plays out across Hampstead, London and Scotland until it reaches a stunning conclusion in the courts of the Old Bailey.

The Mystery of the Downs
When Harry Marsland was caught in a sudden down pour he sought shelter at Cliff Farm. Met at the door by a young woman clearly expecting someone else he is only too glad to get inside to wait out the storm. When they hear a noise upstairs in the deserted house they investigate only to discover the body of the farm's owner, Frank Lumsden, dead of a gunshot wound. Who then, killed Lumsden, and why? Who was the woman expecting and did she have any roll in the murder? These are the questions that private detective Crewe must answer in The Mystery of the Downs.

Visit www.resurrectedpress.com

OTHER RESURRECTED PRESS MYSTERIES

MYSTERIES ON A TRAIN

Before the Orient Express there was:

The Rome Express by Arthur Griffiths
A man is found dead in his first class sleeping compartment on the express from Rome to Paris. Who was his murderer? The Countess? The English General? His brother the clergy man? The maid who has disappeared? Is the French justice system up to solving the crime? Read about it in The Rome Express.

The Passenger from Calais by Arthur Griffiths
Colonel Basil Annesley finds he is the only passenger on the train from Calais to Lucerne. That is until a mysterious woman shows up at the last minute to book a compartment. Who is after her? What is her secret? Is she a criminal or a victim? Read about it in The Passenger from Calais

Visit us at www.resurrectedpress.com

About Resurrected Press

A division of Intrepid Ink, LLC, Resurrected Press is dedicated to bringing high quality, vintage books back into publication. See our entire catalogue and find out more at www.ResurrectedPress.com.

About Intrepid Ink, LLC

Intrepid Ink, LLC provides full publishing services to authors of fiction and non-fiction books, eBooks and websites. From editing to formatting, from publishing to marketing, Intrepid Ink gets your creative works into the hands of the people who want to read them. Find out more at www.IntrepidInk.com.